44
Book Two

Jools Sinclair

Praise for 44...

44
Book Two

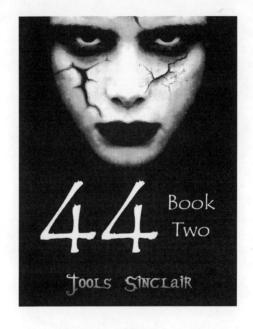

Jools Sinclair

You Come Too Publishing

44 Book Two

Published by You Come Too Publishing, Bend, Oregon.

Text copyright © 2011 by Jools Sinclair.

This book is a work of fiction. Names, characters, places, and incidents are either the product of the author"s imagination or are used fictitiously. Any resemblance to actual persons, living or dead, or to actual events or locales is entirely coincidental.

Printed in the United States of America
First edition, 2011

ISBN-13: 978-1468041880
ISBN-10: 1468041886

for O.

Prologue

It had been more than a year since he had last seen her and his heart ached to be with her again.

The faint sound of drumming seeped across the dark land, invading his thoughts. It was nice though, exotic and gentle, and it soothed him, often lulling him into a light sleep. Sometimes he heard soft voices whispering, telling their stories around the campfires he smelled at night. He found this comforting too.

The day had been long, but not difficult. Basic. Doing the work they expected of him. Nothing special, nothing important.

Most of the time he was able to push away the thoughts of what he had lost. The life he knew. Her. But lately it seemed nearly impossible not to think about it all.

He found himself thinking of her throughout the day as he worked, and at night, always right before drifting off to sleep. He knew he just needed to relax, let the time stretch out a little more. They would be together. It was destiny. They were linked by something greater than both of them. Something that wouldn't allow the vast space between their two worlds to keep them apart. He knew that in his heart and soul. This was all just temporary.

He needed to be more patient and wait for a sign when he could return.

He inhaled sharply and looked up at the dull stars trying to shine through the thick band of haze. The yellow crescent moon kissed the dark sky. It was such a strange land. Dust coated everything, making the night look milky and unnatural.

He rubbed his throbbing temples and waited for sleep to take him. He closed his eyes and thought of her. Her hair, her eyes, her beauty. Her energy. He thought of the times he would walk along the river, breathing in the sweet aroma of the juniper and pine trees, staring at the striking snow-covered mountains in the distance.

They would find each other again, he told himself. They belonged together.

He awoke into the early morning heat, sweat already dripping down his face. He stood up and stared out at the horizon.

Night was always so odd here. Illusive, fast, half-dead. But in the early morning, something lifted. Life began again. The routines and chores of the day replaced the thoughts that ran rampant in the dark.

The large camp was coming to life. Women began cooking at small fires. Babies cried.

He still couldn't shake her from his mind. He walked up to the small, muddy river and kneeled next to it, splashing his face with water.

At least he knew what she was doing in Bend. He had someone there, someone who was watching over her and who reported back to him. Someone who was his eyes and ears until he returned.

Two older men walked toward him on their way to the water for their morning prayers. The plight of the fool, he thought. Thanking this so-called higher power that turned a blind eye while they wallowed in poverty, war, and hunger.

"Good morning, Dr. Mortimer," one of them said, flashing a toothless smile.

He smiled.

He glanced back at the camp. There were so many here on the edge of death, so many who died every day. It had made his job easy. He could do his experiments without that messy part. He didn't have to hurry them along. They presented themselves to him. Death was just a part of life for these people.

And as he discovered, she didn't show up if he didn't kill them. That was an advantage too. Easier for now.

But he still wasn't able to replicate that success he had with her. He needed to get back and find out why his serum had only worked with her. Why she was so special.

His heart fluttered thinking about her. This new emotion he now felt was strong. Powerful. He knew that together they could do incredible things.

A group of young boys wandered down to the shore not far from where he stood, playing with an old soccer ball. It reminded him of her. She loved the game.

He wondered if it was a sign.

He shoved his hands in his pockets, squinting in the sun. A warm, happy feeling shot through him the more he thought about it.

Yes.

It was time to return.

Chapter 1

I took a deep breath, trying to relax.

"Come on, Abby, you can do this," Ty whispered in my ear as the rest of the group headed up the ridge to scout the rapids. I walked slowly behind them. "You've trained for it a long time and you're more than ready. Just loosen up a little."

Ty's shiny, light eyes beamed into mine like he was trying to telepathically shoot me confidence or something. I smiled, battling the bile that was coming up and stinging the back of my throat.

"Thanks," I said.

"You're a great guide," he said in a low voice right before we reached the people waiting on the trail by the river. "Hell, I taught you, of course you're good. But you're a natural too. You'll do fine on this next one."

It's not like this was my first time down the river with the tourists. I had been out here all week. But the first run of the day always shook me up a little.

At the very least I knew I needed to hide my fear a little better. If Ty could see that I was nervous, my group probably would as well.

I pulled down my sunglasses and walked up to them, six somber Japanese tourists, staring at the whitewater with worried faces. I could see that they were really scared.

Dark gray bands of energy hung over them as they stood stiffly next to Ty's rowdy teenagers.

I forced a big smile, hoping it would help. They nodded politely.

I knew Ty was right about me being a natural on the river. I wasn't sure why, but I was pretty good at reading the water and finding the right channels to shoot through, avoiding whirlpools and boulders and downed trees. I had trained for weeks in the spring and beat out more than a dozen other applicants who had been competing for the summer job.

"Okay," Ty said in a loud voice that echoed off the trees and rocks. "Let me have your attention."

I stood next to him as he started talking, the strong smell of the piña colada sunscreen that he always slathered on his arms filling my nostrils.

"This here is Big Eddy, a quarter-mile stretch of continuous class II and Class III plus rapids. This section is the most intense part we'll do out here today, but it's also the most fun."

The teenagers cheered wildly for a minute.

Being able to bring the tourists up on shore to scout the rapids was one of the nice things about this particular river trip. People usually liked studying the raging waves and massive drops down the canyon. Big Eddy was a set of impressive rapids and seeing it was a thrill. It still took my breath away no matter how many times I'd done the run.

Ty pointed out the hidden rocks as he showed everyone the route. He also talked about the small but powerful whirlpool that we needed to avoid.

"Any questions?"

A few hands went up. As Ty answered them, I stared out at the water.

Although it was intense, the run wasn't like a serious river trip. This was more of a tourist attraction. Little kids were even allowed to come. It only took about an hour or so to run the three miles and we did it four times a day. Our job was to make sure the customers had a good time, and then deliver them safely to the take-out point for the bus drivers to shuttle them back down to the resorts in town.

It wasn't the biggest deal that Kate made it out to be sometimes.

"Ready? Let's go!" Ty said as he pulled down his super dark sunglasses that wrapped around his eyes, making him look like an alien.

The other four guides were by the rafts upriver, waiting. They were all friendly enough, but I didn't know them that well. They had all been river rats for the past few years and I was the newbie. Ty was the only one I really talked to.

We headed back to the water. Before taking my seat in the back, I helped Amber hold the raft steady while my group got in. The four women and two men smiled, but they still looked scared. It would probably have been better for them to have not seen Big Eddy up close.

Amber pushed us off and I lined up just behind Ty's raft. My heart thundered in my ears as I grabbed my paddle, staring ahead.

The river immediately picked up speed.

"Okay everybody, remember, this is the fun one!" Ty said, his voice booming over the roar we were paddling into. "Yaw!"

The teenagers' yells bounced off the black lava rocks. I back paddled a bit to give Ty room. My group gripped their paddles, waiting for my instructions.

Ty's raft disappeared into the foam and mist and noise. Wild screams ensued.

"Okay," I shouted. "Everybody ready? Paddles in the water. Plant your feet and paddle hard. Here we go!"

I waited another second or two before paddling, my stomach swaying with each roll of the waves. We were lined up okay, but I was left of where Ty had been, a little off from where I wanted to be.

The river took us, turning white and mean as we dropped and flew over the waves, water splashing into the boat. The current was strong and was trying to push us into the rocks on the right. I tightened my grip and paddled, telling myself I could do this. I could run these rapids. I could beat this water.

"Okay!" I called out. "Right side only."

They listened well and did exactly as we had practiced, the three women on the left pulling out their paddles. The raft evened out as I guided us back into the middle of the channel.

"Good, okay, everybody now!"

The churning water soaked us as we lunged into the next drop, sliding into a wave. We passed the boulder in the middle of the river a little closer than I would have liked, but we were okay.

"Paddles out!"

I pushed my paddle deep into the water and steered us away from the last rock on the left and we dropped again, shooting into the middle of the suddenly calm river.

"Yeah!" I yelled. "Great job everyone!"

My group was all smiles, but unlike everybody else around us, they didn't cheer or high five each other.

Ty gave me a thumbs up without turning around.

The other rafts joined up as we meandered down the canyon, past pine trees and rock cliffs. A crow cawed as it flew above us. I searched for the pair of bald eagles that lived in the trees nearby, but they weren't there.

The hot sun baked my shoulders and a surge of emotion shot through me as I paddled us through the calm stretch. It felt incredible. This was the reason why I was out here on the river every day. With the roar of the rapids at my back and the beauty of the forest all around me, that new feeling swelled up inside.

Peace.

Chapter 2

It had been more than a year since I had seen Jesse.

Thirteen months ago, on a warm May afternoon, we sat by our lake and talked about how we died. His eyes sparkled as he looked at me. And then he kissed me. A long and passionate and sweet kiss. The kiss of dreams. The kiss that you remember forever because it's the one.

And then he vanished.

I turned up the radio and let Adele flood the Jeep with another song about lost love as I waited at a light. Bend was packed with tourists. A large group crossed the street, mothers and kids and two teenage girls in bikinis, their arms wrapped around giant inner tubes, heading to the river.

I had searched everywhere for Jesse. At the basketball courts around town. On the hills of Awbrey Butte and at the parks. I followed every skateboard that scraped the sidewalk. I ran up to tall strangers and I waited outside his house. I lingered around the lake. I drove up to Mt. Bachelor on my own in the winter and searched all the ski runs hoping to find him speeding down the slick slopes with that crazy smile plastered on his face.

But I couldn't find him.

I sighed as I pulled into the parking lot. I got out and walked across the grass.

When we were kids, Jesse and I always came here. It was our park. Sometimes we'd walk over after school and sometimes Kate would drop us off. He played goalie for me and I played one-on-one with him. Or we would just walk around talking while he dribbled his basketball.

It was a good place. I knew he would come here to find me if he could.

I sat down on the cement table, taking a deep breath of the summer air. I watched two kids throwing a Frisbee back and forth as I kicked at the benches. I scanned the play structures, the basketball courts, the fenced-off dog park.

I wasn't going to give up. Jesse was out there somewhere, and I was going to find him.

But sometimes I did wonder if Dr. Krowe, the psychologist I used to see, was right that Jesse had just been a figment of my imagination.

"The mind is an incredible instrument, Abby. It can create whole worlds," he had said during one of our sessions. He had helped me a lot back when I was recovering. I was having a hard time, lost in a dark place.

"Don't you see?" he continued. "You invented Jesse. You loved him and couldn't accept his death so your mind protected you through your trauma. It's a miracle, really. Have you ever thought of what might have happened if you hadn't had Jesse with you all those months? That maybe you wouldn't have made it back psychologically? Having him around you in those transitional months probably saved you. And you must know that Jesse vanishing at the exact same time that you realized he had died is not a mere coincidence."

Dr. Krowe was good people. I knew that. When I woke up after being dead for 44 minutes, I was a mess. I couldn't see colors anymore, play soccer, or remember things. And then I started having terrifying dream-like visions of a serial killer. Dr. Krowe helped me deal with all that. And even though I still lived in a black and white world, most everything else was a lot better. He helped me out of the darkness.

But he was wrong about Jesse. Jesse was real. I could feel it.

But I needed to find him.

Jesse wasn't the only ghost I saw. Since the accident, I saw other ones sometimes. They walked around with heavy energies and dark shadows swirling around them. I didn't see them often, just once in a while. They were in crowds, in stores. Walking down busy streets. They stood a little ways from the living, lurking in this world and not willing to let go.

But they looked different than Jesse. Duller. Faded. Sad. And they had these frightening, intense eyes that gave me chills if I stared at them for too long. That's how I knew they were from another world. They had ghost eyes.

The sightings always left me with a bad feeling afterwards. I tried to ignore them, ducking into stores or turning around and walking the other way. I didn't know why I was seeing them and I didn't care.

There was only one ghost I wanted to find.

I flashed back to when I saw Jesse in the hospital room, standing over my bed right after the doctors brought me back to life. He didn't have his baseball cap on and his eyes were large with worry. I hadn't even recognized him. But then he spoke.

"Craigers," he said, leaning down and whispering. "I'm so glad you made it back."

I had made it back from death to be with him.

And it took me nearly a year to figure out that he wasn't even here.

My phone buzzed. It was Kate, calling to let me know she would be home for dinner.

A heavy surge of sadness rushed through me as I walked back to the car. The engine started along with Adele, always willing to share my sorrow.

Chapter 3

The house was hot and stuffy when I got home. I threw down my bag and flipped on the air conditioning. After taking a quick shower, I headed to the kitchen.

I had started cooking a few months ago after getting hooked on the *Food Network*. At first I made simple things, like steak and mashed potatoes and omelets and spaghetti. But then I went to the library and checked out cookbooks and started trying more complicated recipes. Lately, most of the dinners turned out pretty well.

There was something special about cooking, about chopping onions and fresh Italian parsley and smelling the different spices. Florence and the Machine sautéed on the stereo while I did the same thing to the garlic. The sweet aroma flooded the house.

I read over the recipe once more, double checking that I hadn't missed anything before putting the glass dish into the oven. Then I sat at the counter skimming over other recipes in the cookbook and looking out the window. After about half an hour, I peeked in at the chicken parmesan penne bake. It was bubbling and almost done.

I was trying to do more things around the house to help out. Kate was still a little mad about the river guide job and I was hoping that the dinners would help smooth things over.

"Christ, Abby, couldn't you have just found a summer job serving coffee or something?" she had said when I told her that I had been hired. "I mean, seriously. Why would someone with your history do something like that? I totally don't understand."

She had a point. It wasn't logical and maybe it was even a little insane. Most drowning victims probably didn't want to go anywhere near water ever again. And with everything Kate had gone through while I recovered, she had a right to be angry.

But I had to do it.

I tried to explain to her why I liked being on the river every day. I told her that sometimes I didn't understand it either, but that the dark lake where I drowned had taken something from me and being on the river allowed me to take back some of what I had lost.

"Forget it, Abby. I'm putting my foot down on this," she had said, her eyes wild.

She must have been thinking I was still a kid or something.

I took the job anyway. She didn't speak to me for a few days, but after a little while she let it go. She still didn't like it, but at least we didn't fight about it anymore. Sometimes I felt guilty. I didn't like for her to worry. But it was where I belonged.

"Smells amazing in here," Kate yelled as she dropped her keys on the entryway table.

"Hey, Kate."

Her heels clicked quickly towards the kitchen across the wood floor.

"Can't wait to eat," she said, patting my shoulder on her way to the fridge.

She swung open the wide door and stared inside for a long time before grabbing a small bottle of water.

As always, she looked great even after working all day. Her hair had been growing out and was pulled up loosely on top of her head.

"Good day?" I asked, closing the cookbook.

She drained half the bottle.

"Eh," she said. "That trial is long and boring. It's hard to sit on those uncomfortable benches for hours and then head back to the paper and write up the story for deadline. But I guess it's coming along. I'm hoping they'll wrap up next week. How 'bout you? Good day?"

"Yeah, it was good," I said.

She slid off her shoes.

"What are we having, by the way?"

"One should never ask," I said, quoting from a favorite movie. "It spoils the surprise."

"Thanks, Hannibal. Guess I'll just have to wait to see then."

I got up and checked on dinner after she left. A nice, crusty brown layer had formed on top so I pulled it out of the oven.

I served the penne on fancy white dinner plates with gold rims and put them out on the table with a bottle of white wine and a corkscrew. Kate appeared a minute later in sweats and a T-shirt and sat down.

"This looks great," she said, inhaling the thick steam rising up.

She took the freshly-grated parmesan cheese I had put out and sprinkled some on the pasta while I uncorked the wine and poured her a glass. I served myself some sparkling water.

"To the chef," she said and we toasted our glasses together.

She took a bite.

"Delicious."

I agreed. It was really good. The flavors had come together nicely.

Within a few minutes she had finished and sat back in the chair.

"Want some more?" I asked.

"No, let's see if that holds," she said. "But thanks. It's really nice coming home to this. You've sure become quite the cook."

After a few minutes, we headed over to the living room and turned on the TV. Kate flipped through the channels, stopping at a news feature on CNN about a famous old basketball player who had written a book about depression.

"So, you had a good day?" she asked again, rubbing her face.

"Yeah," I said.

"And that Ty guy? How's he doing?"

It wasn't like I had talked that much about Ty to Kate or anything, but she always asked about him ever since we bumped into him at Safeway one night. She didn't understand about Jesse.

I could see the wheels turning in her head.

"He's good," I said. "Of course, Ty's the type who is always good."

"Yeah, he seems like a happy guy," she said. "Does he have a girlfriend?"

"No," I said. "I think he just got out of a relationship. At least that's what I hear him tell the girls back at the office when they throw themselves at him."

Kate smiled.

"Have you thought about going out with him?"

She did this a lot, especially lately. I knew she was concerned that I was still in love with a dead boy and wanted me to move on. There was no use in trying to explain anymore, so I kept things vague.

"Maybe," I said. "But everyone seems to be after Ty as it is. I don't think I would have a chance."

"Nonsense. You guys would make a great couple. Why don't you invite him over for one of your dinners?"

"That seems a little crazy."

She threw her feet up on the coffee table and stared at the ceiling. I watched the gray waves dance around her.

That was one thing I had gotten really good at this past year. I was able to see other people's moods, see how they were really feeling inside. Now I saw everybody's energy all the time, whether they were friends, bosses, or strangers I passed on the street. Those waves were just a part of them, attached like their sweaters or jackets or faces. It was overwhelming and draining after a while.

But sometimes it was good information to have. Like with the tourists in my raft. I liked knowing if they were feeling scared or cocky or bored. The energy I saw didn't lie.

And, of course, I didn't mind seeing them around the people I knew, like Kate.

But I had to be careful, especially with her. She didn't exactly like it, me knowing how she felt about everything. So I was quiet, never saying much about what I saw and waiting until she was ready to talk to me.

Kate flipped through the channels again.

"Oh, I got a message from Ben today."

Dr. Ben Mortimer had brought me back to life after I died. Kate dated him while I was recovering. But when I started having visions about his brother Nathaniel killing people, everything went to hell.

Nathaniel had murdered four people in Bend. He of course didn't see it that way. They had been sacrificed for the greater good. He said he had invented an antidote that when injected into people who had just died, could bring them back to life. Nathaniel told me he had given me the serum after I had been declared dead at the hospital. He said that I was his first and only success.

Although we confronted Nathaniel one snowy night at Dr. Mortimer's house, he escaped and left Bend without ever facing murder charges. But he told me he would be back for me. He said he would need me to continue his research.

We hadn't heard from Nathaniel since that night, and no one knew where he was. He had resigned from his job back East and had vanished into thin air.

Kate never forgave Dr. Mortimer for letting Nathaniel get away. They broke up shortly after and she had barely spoken to him since.

"What did Dr. Mortimer say?" I asked.

"He wants to see us."

Her energy changed, moving quickly and turning into deep blacks and bright whites. It was always like that when she talked about him. She was surrounded by wild, turbulent waves that I guessed was love, and also hate. It made me a little sad, watching the intense emotions swell up around her.

Unlike Kate, I still kept in touch with Dr. Mortimer through emails and phone calls. Once in a while I even stopped by the hospital and visited him during his breaks, just to say hi.

Kate was angry because Dr. Mortimer had suspected his brother was killing people for his medical experiments long before we had put it together. She believed that if Dr. Mortimer had stopped him when he first realized what was going on, his last victim might still be alive.

Over the past year I tried talking to her about it and tried to get her to see things from his perspective. And it seemed like that was never going to happen. But just when I thought that she would never speak to him again, she started answering his emails. They were still an ocean away from each other emotionally, though. And now that she was with Colin, I doubted they would ever get back together.

"So have you talked to Ben lately?" Kate asked.

It didn't bother her that I still talked to him. In fact, she told me that I should, that Dr. Mortimer saved my life and that he was a real friend. He was someone I could always count on.

"Maybe a month ago."

"He wants to take us out to dinner," she said. "But I don't know. Maybe you two should just go. I don't see the point of me going."

I flashed back on the Thanksgiving we had a few years back, how he came over and how everyone was so happy. I really missed him. He was still like family.

"Kind of weird to invite us out like that, all of a sudden," I said. "Do you think something has happened?"

Kate yawned as she pulled down the blanket from the back of the sofa, wrapping it around her. I had left the air conditioning on high while I was cooking and now the house was too cold. I got up and adjusted the thermostat.

"I don't know, yeah, maybe," she said. "I actually talked to him on the phone. Probably gave him a heart attack, picking up like that. I can't remember the last time we spoke. But he seemed pretty happy, so I don't think it's too serious."

"Gosh, you think? You mean he was actually happy that you talked to him after a year?"

She smiled at me and kicked my foot.

"Don't be snide," she said. "Besides, it hasn't been a year. I saw him at that hospital charity thing in the spring. Anyway, I'm hoping that he has some good news. You know. About *him*."

We always avoided saying Nathaniel's name out loud.

"Yeah," I said.

Since Nathaniel had fled, Dr. Mortimer had been trying to find him, although so far he hadn't had any luck. I believed him when he told us that he would search the world for his brother, but I could tell Kate still had her doubts. She said it was just human nature to protect family and while she understood that, she expected more from him.

"You can't protect a killer," she had said often.

And she was right. But, while he may have hesitated at first, I didn't think Dr. Mortimer was doing that now.

Maybe he was worried about her getting too serious with Colin. Last time I saw him, he asked me about their relationship.

"I guess there could be news," I said.

Kate was quiet for a moment.

"Would you mind just going by yourself? I don't know if I can face him quite yet."

"Come on," I said. "You should come too. It's really not such a big deal. It's just a dinner."

And he did save my life, I thought. It seemed to me like we owed him. She sighed, like she had read my mind.

"Okay. You're right. No big deal."

"Good. And don't worry. I'll provide the sparkling conversation."

"It's going to be a long night then."

Kate was always joking about my conversation skills because I essentially had none. While she would walk into a room full of strangers and have a dozen new friends on her Facebook account within an hour, I would be in the corner petting the cat. We were different like that. I didn't even have a Facebook account.

I wasn't sure if my awkward social skills were because of the accident or not. When I came back from being dead, a lot of people started treating me different. They thought I was a freak, blessed and cursed at the same time. And living in a small city, my story had gotten around. It felt like everybody knew about what had happened. They would stare at me with large eyes, suspicious of where I had been when I had died and what I had seen.

But it was finally getting better. In the last few months a veil had lifted and I was becoming more comfortable with who I was. People were leaving me alone too. It helped that I was free from high school. Away from old friends who I now scared or who just hated me.

"Yeah, okay," Kate said. "We'll do dinner. Can you go next Friday? We can meet up after work over at the The Old Mill."

"Sure."

I was happy she decided to come.

After he had escaped, I promised that I would always tell Kate about any new visions. And I kept that promise. Since the college instructor, I never had another one of Nathaniel killing anyone.

But I did have feelings about him sometimes, especially as I drifted off to sleep. Murky and dark, like he was watching from far away. I knew he was out there somewhere, lying low, still working on his research. I figured that as long as he was far away, I didn't have to tell anyone. There was no use stirring all that up again.

"Okay, I'll let Ben know," Kate said.

"Good."

It was silly, but I was kind of excited that we were all going to be together again.

It had been a long time.

Chapter 4

It felt great to be able to play soccer again.

To be out on the field, kicking a ball toward goal was one of the best feelings in the world. Those terrible memories of sitting on the bench in my senior year and watching my varsity team play without me were slowly eroding. Dr. Mortimer had been right. My body healed. It just took time.

It's not like I was as good as I used to be, good enough to get a college scholarship or anything. I was just playing on a Parks and Rec team, made up mostly of 30- and 40-year-olds. There were a few people my age, but not many.

Our games were on Tuesday and Thursday nights in the summer league, sometimes late and under the bright lights. And even though I was playing with and going up against a bunch of rec players, I was getting better. I was dribbling and scoring and we were winning. Like old times.

And I was even making a few friends.

I walked up to the sidelines, dropped my soccer bag down on the grass, and took out my ball.

"How ya doing, AC?" Jack Martin asked as he walked up to me smiling.

He usually called everyone by their initials.

"Hey, Jack. I'm good."

Jack was obsessed with soccer. He played on three different teams with a game every night of the week. He loved Real Madrid and DVR'd a lot of the Spanish league games, inviting the team over for soccer parties on the weekends. He was friendly and outgoing, but didn't have that insane white energy surrounding him like Ty. Everybody liked Jack and he seemed to know all the players on all the teams.

"Another new jersey?" I said, checking my shoelaces.

He showed off the Real Madrid shirt and then turned around, modeling it. I cringed. I was a Barcelona fan.

"Just came today."

We walked to the center of the field for the kickoff. The ref blew the whistle and we started the game.

"Give it to Abby, she's open," I heard Tim yell a few minutes in.

Bree passed me the ball and I took it in and shot hard, but the goalie had time to get in position and plucked it out of the air.

"Good try, AC," Jack yelled from midfield.

Some of the players were brutal. Something about rec soccer seemed to bring out the worst in some people. High school girls could be clumsy, but this was beyond that. As they worked through their issues, some of these players became aggressive and crossed lines. Mostly large, overweight men in their 40s desperate to prove something to themselves and anyone who got in their way. It was dangerous out here and I was surprised there weren't more injuries.

There were two of those guys on the team we were playing now. Fortunately I was a lot faster, but I still had to keep my eyes open and watch my back.

As I ran back, I noticed Kate and Colin were standing on the sidelines. It made me happy to see her there, watching me play. She waved and I waved back.

At the half, we were tied 0-0. Jack walked with me and I introduced him to my sister and her boyfriend.

"She's a great player," Jack said before leaving to get water.

Kate smiled.

"Wow, Abby. I still can't believe you're playing again. I love being out here watching you," Kate said.

"Thanks for coming," I said. "You too, Colin."

He nodded.

Colin was always a little shy around me and usually didn't say too much. I could tell that he was uncomfortable too. I figured Kate told him my story and it made him nervous. But at least he didn't ask any questions.

The second half was tough but our goalkeeper did a great job. Then, close to the end of the game, Tim sent up a perfect pass and I took the ball in, made my way around the last defender, and shot at the top of the far post, right into the corner of the net.

The team erupted in shouts and cheers as I jumped up and down screaming. I guessed I had something to prove too. It was a sweet goal. Tim, Jack, and Bree came running up and gave me high fives.

The game ended a few seconds later.

"What a great goal!" Kate said, handing me my bottle of Gatorade and patting my back.

"Remarkable," Colin said.

"Thanks. And thanks again, you guys, for being here."

Kate rubbed my sweaty head as we walked to the car.

Colin was about her height and had light hair and an angular jaw and serious eyes. He was both smart and ambitious like her, but didn't laugh or smile much, and was a little smug. I hadn't spent that much time with them, but the few times we did hang out, they usually ended up talking about local politicians and city events. There was never too much fun in their conversations. It seemed kind of stressful.

"I bet it feels great being back out on the field," Kate said, as we weaved out of the way of cars leaving the parking lot in a mad frenzy.

"It does," I said.

I unlocked the Jeep.

"Wait. I'll ride home with you. I have to grab my stuff. I'll be right back," she said.

Colin said goodbye and they walked over to his Precis.

I watched them for a minute. They just didn't seem quite right for each other. There was no balance. And just like I could see if people were in love, I could also see when they weren't.

Kate walked up, opened the car door, and threw her stuff in the back.

"Okay, ready Eddie," she said.

I started the engine and pulled out onto the street.

It was warm and there was still a little light in the sky, with the edges of a few clouds lit up. It must have been a really nice sunset, but Kate didn't mention it.

"I was a little worried for you during the game. That beast was after you, trying to take you down," she said.

She pulled out her phone and checked it.

"Yeah," I said. "Good thing I have some of my speed back."

"The ref should have red carded him and thrown him out. I saw him trip that girl with the blonde hair."

She fiddled with the radio and unrolled the window. Josh Ritter started singing about a lantern and lost sheep growing teeth.

Kate yawned, resting her head against her arm.

"How are you doing?" I asked, glancing over at her.

"Fine. I'm just tired."

I nodded.

"How's everything with Colin?"

"Oh, okay. I know you can probably see that I'm not in love with him or anything."

I was quiet.

"I mean, not yet, anyway. But maybe I'll grow to love him. I like him a lot. He's smart and interesting and ambitious. Not a loafer, which is always good."

I flashed back on one of her old boyfriends and smiled.

"Matt!" we said together, laughing.

Last time Kate had heard from Matt, the artist and professional moocher, he was living in a commune in northern California with his girlfriend and had a baby on the way.

I turned up our street and pulled into the driveway.

"What a great thing," Kate said as she grabbed all her stuff from the backseat. "You playing soccer again."

I followed her up the steps to the porch and inside, smiling.

It was.

Chapter 5

The sun beat down as we pushed off into the last run.

It had been a good day. I steered us through the rapids, hitting all the right channels, and there were no close calls. The customers had been good too. They were friendly and excited about going down the river. Even the group of teenagers had been surprisingly tolerable.

On the last run, I had three couples. They asked questions about Bend and how long I had been a guide. I told them the truth. It didn't seem to bother them that I was new. We talked about the various wildlife in the area and then about the weather.

We pulled off to scout the river like we always did. Amber and the others led everybody on the short trail to the Big Eddy viewpoint. Ty and I stayed back with the rafts in the shade. It was hot, but a nice breeze blew into us off the water.

"So, Abby, when are you going out to dinner with me?" Ty said out of the blue. He was wearing those dark sunglasses so I couldn't tell if he was joking.

My stomach did a backflip. I was trying to think of something clever to say. Luckily before I had a chance to respond, a little kid ran up to him and asked for help tightening his life vest.

"I'll need an answer by the end the day," Ty said.

I smiled nervously. I hadn't expected it and wasn't really sure what it meant. Maybe it was just like a get-together for burgers after work with the other guides. I hoped so.

We launched into the main channel and I straightened us up. The current was clipping us from the left, but I steered through it and we shot Big Eddy nicely. Large waves crashed in, soaking everybody, but it made them happy. It was a perfect day for getting drenched.

At the pick-up point, we pulled in and said good bye. The happy, wet tourists thanked us as they headed toward the bus, some coming back down and giving us tips. I got a few. I watched as a middle-aged guy in khaki shorts approached Ty and shook his hand, slipping him a bill.

"Thanks so much, I really appreciate it," he said.

Ty walked over to me and we watched the bus pull out onto the dirt road, a cloud of dust rising behind it.

"Ha! Looks like I'll be having a sweet weekend," he said, snapping the $20 bill in front of me.

"As always, Mr. Tips."

"Aw, I've been watching you raking it in," he said. "I saw those families float some love your way."

"Not like you," I said, smiling and bowing my head. "You are the master."

None of it really mattered because it was the policy among the guides to pool all the tips at the end of the day and split them six ways. It was Ty's idea, even though he was always the one who pulled in the most money.

He stared at me for a moment and I wondered if he was waiting for an answer about going to dinner. I was hoping that somebody would walk up. Then he suddenly grabbed some paddles and headed to the van.

When he returned, he eyed my arms.

"Not bad," he said. "You're getting there, Abby Craig. By the end of the summer your arms will be like mine."

He flexed his muscles.

I shook my head.

"Well, let's hope not," I said.

I didn't plan on looking like a wrestler.

It was true though, that between the river and soccer, I was getting in pretty good shape. It had been a long time since I had felt strong. It gave me confidence about steering the raft away from the obstacles in the river.

We loaded the gear with the other guides and pulled up the rafts. The dry afternoon air felt good and I was glad the day was over. I was tired. I headed back down to help pull out the last raft.

Ty came up and started kicking at the river like it was a soccer ball, getting me all wet. He was such a goofball sometimes, especially at the end of the day. I cupped my hands together and scooped up water and threw it at him. We were both knee deep in the river and it felt good.

I slammed the water with both hands with all my strength, soaking Ty. He laughed.

"Okay, now you're really in trouble," he said.

He suddenly picked me up and tossed me in. But as I fell under the water, it all came back.

I was drowning again.

I couldn't breathe and was sinking in the dark water down, down, down to the bottom. Panic ripped through me. My heart raced as I tried to hold my breath, tried not to inhale death. I started screaming, trying to push up toward the surface. But the darkness had a hold on me again. And it was trying to pull me down.

Suddenly an arm wrapped around my waist and lifted me up above the surface. I gasped to breathe, coughing up water. Ty helped me to the shore and I fell down to the ground as I sputtered and choked.

"You're okay," he said, slapping my back.

Amber and Jake ran up, looking on with worried eyes.

I finally caught my breath and stopped coughing.

"I'm fine," I said.

"I'm so sorry," Ty said.

He sat down next to me and put his arm on my shoulder.

"You know I was just joking, right? It was just meant to be fun."

He kept staring at me. It was the first time I had seen him so serious and upset.

"Really. I'm fine," I said, gently pushing him away and forcing a smile.

Most of the water was out of my lungs now and I was suddenly embarrassed. Amber and Jake both gave me an odd look and walked away.

I hadn't been sure if they knew about me, but now watching their expressions, I was positive they did. They probably thought it was insane for someone like me to have this job.

I stood up.

"Just breathed in a little water," I said. "I'm good to go. Sorry, Ty. You just caught me off guard, that's all."

I pretended to punch him in the gut.

"But revenge will be mine," I said, forcing another smile.

Ty smiled back, cautiously. Gray waves surrounded him. He was quiet for a minute. I figured he probably knew about me too.

"You sure you're okay?" Ty said.

"I'm all right, nobody worry about me," I said, quoting from the *Caddyshack* song.

"Sorry, Abby. It was such a stupid thing to do," he said. "I just, well, wasn't thinking."

He gave me hug.

He smelled good, like always, full of tropical sunscreen and river water and pine trees and sun. He smelled like summer. When we pulled away, I saw that he was back to the bright white waves that usually surrounded him.

"Let's finish this up and get outta here," he said. "Take a few moments though."

He walked up toward the bus carrying a stack of life vests.

I took a deep breath and walked back over to the edge of the water. I reminded myself that everything was okay, that I was safe. That nothing bad happened.

And that's when I saw her.

Floating above the river, not more than 30 feet away, she stood dressed in a long white gown, staring at me with icy eyes.

I jumped back, my heart hammering in my chest and fear shooting through my body.

She just hovered there, above the current, her eyes drilling into me. Chills ran up and down the back of my neck, but I couldn't turn away. It was impossible to ignore this ghost. I just stood there.

I heard soft footsteps in the gravel behind me. It was Amber picking up the last of the paddles.

"Sorry," she said loudly, smiling. "Didn't mean to startle you."

When I looked back at the water, the ghost was gone.

That familiar old dread swept through me like a tsunami, swift and fast and with no mercy. I stood there at the edge of the water for a while, numb and sick, trying not to vomit.

Chapter 6

I wasn't going to tell Kate about the ghost.

Not yet anyway. Maybe it would be a one-time thing like the others. Maybe I had invented her. Maybe she wasn't real.

I pulled up into the downtown parking lot and found a spot facing Drake Park. I got out and walked over to the edge of the plaza and did a quick scan, looking for Jesse.

I missed having a best friend. This was the kind of thing I could have talked to him about. Even if he thought I was crazy, it always felt safe to tell Jesse anything. And he always gave me honest feedback. I could tell him all my secrets.

I scanned the groups of people hanging out in the park, but Jesse wasn't there. I walked over to Wall Street.

Kate and I were meeting downtown to go shopping. I didn't really feel like going, but I didn't want to cancel at the last minute. Besides, I needed a new pair of sandals and there was a sale at one of the shoe stores. I would have to hide the fear that was still churning inside me from her. But that wasn't always so easy to do.

I saw her Subaru parked in the lot and figured she was probably in her favorite store. I started walking over in that direction and a minute later found her in the back at the racks.

"Hey, Abby!"

"Hey, Kate. Finding anything?"

I breathed slowly and deeply as I looked through the clothes, trying to calm down. She pulled out a gray suit jacket. I was sure I'd seen a bunch of the exact same ones hanging in her closet.

"Maybe. What do you think?" she said, turning it around and holding it up so I could see.

"Yeah," I said. "It's nice."

I didn't even own one of those types of jackets and I hoped that whatever I ended up doing, I would never need one. I was happy going to work in river sandals and water-resistant shorts and T-shirts.

I waited while she tried it on in front of a mirror. It was a nice fit.

"Oh, never mind," she said, putting it back on the rack. "I have a few of these already anyway. Let's go."

We walked outside into the heat and down the street. The sidewalk was crowded. There was a good chance I might recognize someone from the rafting trips, but I didn't care. It was nice to be walking around.

"I need a coffee," Kate said. "I have to go back to work later. Want one?"

"Sure," I said.

We turned down Minnesota and walked into Thump.

I always liked our regular coffee house. It had a good atmosphere and we had gotten to know the employees. The brick walls were decorated with local art and had a lot character. Kate and I came here often.

I sat at a small table in the back and waited while she ordered and brought back our usuals.

"Thanks," I said.

We both talked about our days. She hesitated and studied me when I told her that I had a great day. Kate was always pretty good at picking up on lies, but she let it go.

"So we have our dinner this week with Dr. Mortimer, right?" I said playing with my cup. "You're still coming, right?"

Kate hadn't said anything about it recently and I hoped she wasn't thinking of blowing it off.

"Oh, yeah," she said. "No big deal, like you said. It'll be fine."

She had a lot of those little gray waves moving quickly around her suddenly. She was nervous. I was glad she was still willing to go.

Her phone buzzed and she stopped to read it, but didn't say anything.

Someone came in and Kate waved.

"One of the TV reporters from the trial," she said. "We sit next to each other all day on those stupid, hard benches. My butt is killing me. Tomorrow I'm bringing a pillow."

I smiled.

"When was the last time you actually saw Ben?" she asked.

"End of April. I stopped by the hospital and dropped off those cookies I made for him."

"Oh, yeah," she said. "I remember now."

"He says he wants to come watch one of my games," I said. "He's letting me know when he can make it. It's hard since he works nights. I emailed him my soccer schedule a few days ago."

Kate nodded.

"Make sure to tell me when he's coming so Colin and I aren't there on the sidelines. I wouldn't want us all to meet, if you know what I mean."

"Of course," I said.

"Let's continue shopping," Kate said, picking up her paper cup.

We walked out into the sun and headed over to the shoe store. I found a pair of river sandals but they were super expensive, even on sale. I passed on them. I could find something over at Big 5. Kate looked around at the shoes, but I could tell by her face it wasn't her kind of store. There wasn't one pair of high heels in the whole place.

We strolled past the kitchen store and the wine shop and crossed the street, making our way to another clothes store. A shot of cold air greeted us as we opened the door and Kate headed to the back. I stayed up front and checked out the T-shirts and shorts.

It took a minute before I spotted Amanda, looking at clothes in the bins. She must have been back for the summer. The last I heard she was going to college in California. She hadn't seen us come in and I hid in the side aisle, keeping my head down. I didn't want to bump into her and I knew she felt the same.

We had been friends for a long time before the accident and I knew she was a good person deep down. But she had refused to forgive me for being with Jesse on the day he died.

It wasn't even like Jesse and I had done anything. But thinking about it now, I knew it was more complicated than that. I think Amanda sensed that even though they were together, Jesse didn't love her. He still loved me. She must have known it was just a matter of time.

That was my fault because I had waited too long before wanting him. I had waited until she was in love with him and then I made my decision, taking him away from her.

I tried to talk to her before she left for college. I wanted to explain, wanted her to know that I didn't mean to hurt her. It didn't go well. She told me she wouldn't forgive me and probably never could, and that the bottom line was that I had no business being up at the mountain snowboarding with her boyfriend. And that a real friend wouldn't have done that.

And if I hadn't gone up there with him, Jesse might still be alive.

That last part hurt. It was like she had sliced me open and pulled out my heart. Because truthfully, sometimes I wondered about the exact same thing.

"You know, you owed me more than that, Abby," I remembered her saying before she walked away. "That was so wrong."

As I watched her leave that day, it came to me that in some ways this town had broken her too. The fact that Jesse and I were together made for good gossip. Besides dealing with the pain of Jesse's death, Amanda was embarrassed that her boyfriend had been with another girl.

Seeing Amanda now was a reminder of those things I didn't like to think about.

I looked over at Kate who had been trying to get my attention, raising her eyebrows and signaling with her head that we should leave.

"Let's get out of here," she whispered.

We walked out the door.

"She must be back for summer break," I said.

"She's holding grudges. She gave you a real nasty look back there. I would advise to just stay away from her."

Chapter 7

It was another good day on the river. I didn't see the ghost and I was hoping that maybe it was just an isolated incident. After the third run down the rapids, a dad came up and thanked me, handing me a twenty dollar bill. Before putting it in the tip pot at the end of the day, I did a little bragging about it to Ty.

"Of course you got a fat tip," he said matter-of-factly. "You're my protégé. It's all because of me. I've taught you well. That's why I get half."

Ty could always make me laugh. He seemed in an especially good mood lately even though I still hadn't quite figured out what to say about his dinner offer. I wanted whatever I said to sound right and I didn't want to hurt his feelings. I hadn't come up with the right words yet.

We said goodbye and I drove home, got ready, and went back out to The Old Mill for dinner with Kate and Dr. Mortimer. I found her waiting and talking on the phone in front of Greg's Grill, still in her work clothes. She was putting in long hours lately. Other than shopping the other day, I really hadn't seen her much.

I loved eating at this restaurant. We could usually get a table right next to the river.

We followed a young hostess to a table. It was a beautiful summer evening and there were a lot of people out walking on the path near the water. We sat down and looked at the menus.

"This is nice," Kate said. "Just sitting out here. I feel like I haven't been outside in months."

I nodded.

"Did you bring a pillow to the trial today?" I asked, smiling.

"Stadium seat," she said. "Got it at Dick's. It's made a big difference too, but my back is still sore."

I hadn't been following it, but it seemed to be a popular conversation all over Bend. I heard people talking about the trial in the grocery store and at the bank. Even the girls in the office where we signed out had mentioned it to Ty.

"The first of the closing arguments was today, so it's wrapping up. I can't wait. I barely remember what it's like to be on a regular beat. I've been stuck in that courthouse for nearly a month."

"So what's it about anyway?"

"An attorney is being accused of embezzlement. It's a big deal because he was a congressman for twenty years. When he retired, he moved to Bend and opened up a law firm. Personally I think he's guilty, but he's going to walk. I can tell that the jury likes him."

Kate was always good at figuring people out. She didn't see energy or anything, but she seemed to pick up on other things. Maybe it was their body language or the pauses in between their sentences. It was probably why she was such a good reporter.

She sat up in her chair and pulled her sunglasses up to the top of her head. I noticed she was wearing dark purple eye shadow and a little more mascara than usual. Then she pulled them down again.

A canoe paddled past us. A tall man was standing up in the middle, his dog up at the front. The waitress came and asked if we wanted any drinks. Kate ordered a glass of Chardonnay and I got a Cherry Coke.

"Well, at least the trial is almost over," I said.

"Yeah. And I'm getting some good clips for my portfolio. But I'm really looking forward to getting back to my regular beat. I miss it."

My phone buzzed. It was a text from Dr. Mortimer.

"He says he'll be here in 10 minutes."

A brief sadness flashed across Kate's face.

"I wonder how he's doing in the ER," she said. "I mean, if he still likes it and everything. He used to talk about going into private practice. He said he wanted to work with kids, be a pediatrician."

"I don't know," I said. "He doesn't really talk about it to me. Thanks again for coming, Kate. I know it must be hard."

"Nonsense. We know hard. This isn't hard. But don't read more into this. It's just a dinner with an old friend, that's all."

She must have felt like she had to say it, but I wish she hadn't. It felt too sharp, like she had made her decision about him forever. I didn't always understand those thick lines that she drew in the sand when it came to Dr. Mortimer and sometimes it made me mad. Here they were, both in love with each other and yet she refused that love, buried it deep, locked it up, and threw away the key. I would give anything to have Jesse with me now. And I wouldn't have cared what he had done or what he hadn't done. I loved him with all my heart.

"I know," I said. "You don't have to tell me that. It's just nice, the three of us having dinner."

She stared at me for a minute, her hair blowing around her face. I could see her sad eyes through her lightly-tinted movie-star sunglasses.

"Sorry, didn't mean to get bitchy. I'm just tired. Here's to weekends," Kate said, lifting her water glass.

I raised mine and we tapped them together and sipped.

The waitress came back. She looked familiar but I couldn't place her. Our eyes met for a moment and she smiled. Maybe from school. I wasn't sure. Kate told her we were waiting for someone.

"You know, Abby, you're looking good. You got that nice outdoorsy tan going and a healthy glow."

"Thanks," I said.

I was also letting my hair grow long, like when I was a kid. Most of the time I had it back in a ponytail, but when I let it down like tonight, it was half way down my back.

"So I'm glad. If being a river guide is making you happy, good. You deserve it. I'll be relieved when the season is over, but it's nice seeing you like this."

I smiled. I did feel happier lately and was glad Kate was able to see it. Maybe it would help her to stop worrying so much about me.

Her expression suddenly turned serious.

It was easy to figure it out. Dr. Mortimer must have arrived.

Chapter 8

Kate stood up with a strained smile spread across her face. I heard his voice behind me.

"Kate and Abby," he said.

I turned around. Dr. Mortimer was smiling that great smile he had, the one that made his eyes look all crinkly.

"Hi, Ben," Kate said as she walked around me.

White and dark waves surrounded them both and I walked up to them.

"Hello, old friend," he said to me.

Dr. Mortimer was as handsome as ever. His hair was a little lighter than the last time I'd seen him and he had a dark tan that made his eyes stand out even more than usual. He was wearing a button-down shirt and khakis. He looked like he had stepped out of an REI catalog, stylish and ready for an adventure.

"Kate, you look beautiful. And Abby. Look at you! You look great," he said. "Just great. It's so good to see you two. It's been too long."

There was a brief, awkward silence after he said that, but he was right. It had been too long. We sat down.

"Yeah," I said finally, grasping for words.

I hoped Kate could speak up and be her typical charming self, but she was unusually quiet. It was up to me, at least for now.

"So, how is the ER?" I asked.

"Good, good," he said, still smiling and staring at Kate. "The same, but it's good."

I glanced over and saw the mix of dark and light energy around her. Her face was tense, like she was having a private conversation in her head, trying to talk down those feelings that were surging up around her.

The waitress brought Dr. Mortimer a menu and a glass of water and asked if he wanted a drink.

"Oh, sure. I'll take a glass a wine. Whatever she's having," he said, pointing to Kate. "Thanks."

We sat quiet for a moment, a soft summer breeze blowing around us. It was great to see him, even better than I had expected. He still felt part of the family, even with everything. I studied him for a minute while he looked at the menu.

"I'm so sorry I'm late. I got stuck at work. Have you ordered yet?"

"Not yet," Kate said.

"I think I'll treat myself to a steak," he said, putting the menu down. "Abby. Let's start with you. Tell me what you've been up to this summer."

I talked about soccer and cooking for a while. Then I spilled it and told him about the river guide job, focusing mostly on the friendly people I met, and how great it was being outside in nature all day.

He looked a little distressed, but I couldn't blame him. He took his napkin and put it in his lap.

"A river guide, eh? That's an interesting choice."

He then smiled at Kate.

"Don't look at me," she said. "It wasn't my idea."

He nodded. I could tell he didn't really like it either, but he seemed to understand.

"Just be careful out there."

"I will," I said.

48

"You know, it's hard not to worry. If I had my choice, I wouldn't want you near any sort of water ever again. But I can understand why you're doing it," he said. "So Kate, how's the newspaper biz treating you? Still chasing the big stories I bet."

His eyes danced as he looked at her.

Kate still seemed super stressed out. I didn't know how much wine it might take before she was comfortable around Dr. Mortimer, but the one glass that she was barely drinking from wasn't getting it done. She didn't respond, so I jumped in.

"She's covering that big trial downtown."

It worked. She finally started talking. First about the trial and then about some of the problems at the DA's office.

We ordered dinner. I decided on the bacon cheeseburger and Kate got a steak like Dr. Mortimer. By the time the food arrived, everyone had loosened up a little, the stress lifting away as the sun sank behind Mt. Bachelor.

"Summer jobs can be great," Dr. Mortimer said. "Back when I was an undergrad, I had the best one ever. I worked on a tour boat out of Boston Harbor three summers in a row. It was incredible, being out on the water all day, the salty sea air blowing through my hair as I talked to people about history. I really loved it."

I could see his light energy swirling around him as he spoke.

"I bet your rafting is like that. But tell me what you have planned for the fall," he said. "Any plans? College courses or something?"

I knew they meant well, but I hated that question. Kate asked it a lot.

"No," I said. "Not yet. I'm still trying to figure out what I want to do."

I never told them, but I didn't see the point of going to college. It was such a great feeling when I graduated from high school. It felt like I was free. Released. Senior year was torture, going to class every day, getting C's and D's on tests no matter how hard I studied. And dealing with all those people. I was relieved to be out and never wanted to go back to school.

Everyone was sure that going to college would be the next logical step for me, figuring that if my body was healing so well, my mind must be too. Even Dr. Krowe was pushing it, suggesting that at the very least I should enroll at the local community college until I got some confidence to attend the university.

There was no way I was sitting in a classroom again, trying desperately to pass tests and learn about things I could care less about. I was going to figure something else out.

"I'm not sure what I want to do yet," I said. "Weighing all my options."

I was still a little lost. The river job made me feel better, but it was only for a few more months. I'd have to come up with something soon.

"Don't think you have to figure it all out before you go to college," Dr. Mortimer said. "Most kids your age have no idea what they're going to do with their lives. I sure didn't when I was your age. But if you go, you can take different classes and find out what it is you would like to do."

I sighed and looked out at the mountains, trying not to get frustrated.

"She has time," Kate said.

That surprised me. She was usually pretty adamant about filling out applications and had been pushing me to look into different universities since winter.

"Actually, I've been thinking about it. I think it's smart to figure out what you want first. College is too expensive these days."

"Yeah, I see what you're saying," Dr. Mortimer said. "You're right, Kate. The cost of college is astronomical. And it keeps going up. But I bet Abby could get some assistance. Scholarships or some other help of some sort."

He smiled and I felt my stomach tighten. Good God. We needed to change the subject, and fast.

A group of kids in bright plastic rafts drifted past us, down the river. The restaurant was suddenly loud and busy, packed with people talking and laughing and drinking. Soft jazz drifted between conversations.

I finished up the last of my cheeseburger as they talked more about work and the weather and baseball. Kate was a big Red Sox fan and of course, so was Dr. Mortimer.

"Ben," she said after the plates were cleared, pausing before going on. She sat straight up in her chair. "Any news? About *him*, I mean."

My stomach dropped a few feet. I hated talking about Nathaniel. It always brought up those deep, dark feelings and I couldn't stop flashing back to when I watched him kill those innocent people in my visions.

The police department never charged Nathaniel with the murders. Nor did they officially solve any of them. They decided that the four deaths were unrelated, even though an unknown drug had been found in all the victims' blood. The police chief issued a statement saying that they had been exposed to a "new, lethal drug for sale out on our streets," and that they all had histories of substance abuse. The cases were closed. Nathaniel wasn't even a wanted man, at least not in Bend.

"Yes, well, there is actually some news about him, in a way," Dr. Mortimer said. He cleared his throat and took a sip of his espresso. "I've found out a few things. First of all, Nathaniel is out of the country and has been for many months. Maybe even a year. I wanted to tell you two that so you can stop worrying. He's in Africa."

"Africa?" Kate asked.

"We don't know where exactly yet. But we're very close to finding him. I've hired a top detective firm and they're confident they'll have his exact location soon."

Kate nodded and then sighed heavily.

Dr. Mortimer looked at me, then back at Kate, his face flattening a little. He could see she wanted more.

"We've traced him to an organization called Doctors Without Borders."

"Really?" she said, coming back to life a bit.

"What is that?" I asked.

"It's a group of doctors and nurses who go all over the world to provide medical care to people," Dr. Mortimer said. "And the agency thinks that he's joined them."

He finished his coffee and waited for a reaction. But Kate said nothing. She was probably disappointed, wanting instead to hear that Nathaniel had been caught somewhere in Boston and was going to jail. Or something like that.

The silence steeped like a teabag. No one said anything, even though it was growing uncomfortable.

"Well, at least he's far away," I said, finally.

"Ben, that doesn't sound like your brother," Kate said. "I mean, helping people and actually practicing medicine."

Dr. Mortimer nodded.

"I can see what you're saying. But before he lost his mind, he really was a very good doctor. Maybe he's gone back to that and stopped doing research."

Kate gave him a sarcastic look.

52

"But what matters is that we're close to finding him and it shouldn't be too long," he said. "Look, I know I should have done more back when I found out about him. But I'm determined to make this right now."

Kate glanced over at me.

"I'll find him. I won't let you down. Not again. I promise."

Kate nodded, the lights from the restaurant casting shadows on her face.

"But then what, Ben?" she asked. "It's a nice gesture and all, but I don't see what you'll do after. There were no charges filed against him. He got away clean. So what happens after you find him?"

Dr. Mortimer rubbed his face.

"I don't know yet," he said. "But somehow I'll find a way to bring him to justice."

The wind blew into us and the umbrella tilted, looking like it was almost going to fall, before regaining its balance.

"As long as you're seriously looking for him, don't forget about Abby. Maybe she could help you out," Kate said.

My heart raced. I wasn't expecting that and Dr. Mortimer looked at me with a strange expression on his face.

"What does she mean?" he asked, staring at me.

"Those dreams. The visions of your brother that she used to get. Remember?"

Dr. Mortimer looked both concerned and annoyed, like he didn't want to think about all that again.

"Have you had any more of those?" he asked, turning toward me.

"No," I said, just above a whisper.

"I'm just saying that Abby should be part of this," Kate said. "And that you need to know if she has another vision.

They were real, Ben. I was there. For better or worse, she seems to have a connection to him in that way. She can help you."

I didn't know why Kate was saying all this. I hadn't had one vision since Nathaniel had left town last year. But she seemed adamant about it. Dr. Mortimer sat back in his chair, darker energy above him.

"Okay," he said. "Abby, have you had any dreams or feelings at all about him lately?"

I could tell he still wasn't sure about any of it, but unlike Kate, I didn't take it personally. Dr. Mortimer was a man of medicine, a scientist. I knew he wasn't too interested in all that psychic stuff I went through. But it didn't matter to me. He had saved my life.

Kate was being hard on him and I wished she would let up a little.

"No, nothing," I said.

"Look. We're all on the same page here," he said. "I do want to hear about anything you think is important regarding Nathaniel because I think everything will help. I want us all to work together."

Kate inhaled, but then smiled. It was a real smile for the first time that night.

"Good. I'm glad you realize that it's not silly to use Abby to help catch him."

"Okay, good," he said. "I'll keep you updated with anything that comes in. I promise."

Dr. Mortimer stared out at the sunset while Kate finished her espresso.

"So how's that new boyfriend of yours?" he asked.

I was surprised at the question and Kate looked flustered for a moment. She put down her cup and paused, struggling to find the right words.

"Oh. Colin," she said, trying to sound casual. "He's good."

I could tell that Kate was wondering how he knew about Colin as her eyes rested on mine for a moment.

"You'd like him," she added.

Dr. Mortimer smiled.

"I'm sure he's a nice guy. Good. Good for you."

I figured he just wanted back into our lives, one way or another. And maybe by accepting that Kate had moved on, we could all be friends again.

I waited for her to ask if he was seeing anyone, but she didn't. We stared at couples and kids in bright shirts walking along the path. Kate's phone buzzed and she stood up and answered it, walking over to the grass as she talked. Dr. Mortimer asked the waitress for the check and handed her his credit card.

"Thanks, Dr. Mortimer," I said. "Dinner was great,"

"My pleasure. I hope we can do this again. More often, I mean."

He stood up and stretched.

"I promise you," he then said. "I'll find him. And he'll be held accountable for all the terrible things he's done, regardless of the police department's theory." I could see the hurt in his eyes, the betrayal he felt. Embarrassment, too. "I won't let anything happen to you."

I nodded.

Kate finished her conversation and joined us again as he signed for the bill. She thanked him for dinner and they said goodbye. I saw those crazy bands of white energy shooting out around both of them. I gave them a moment and walked over to the edge of the river, looking for Jesse. It was an old habit.

I didn't know why, but it seemed like he should have been here with us. A sharp sadness jolted through me. I wiped a tear that had slipped down my cheek, pulled down my sunglasses, and turned back toward Kate and Dr. Mortimer, who were making awkward small talk.

"Maybe we could do this again before the summer is over?" he said.

"Yeah, maybe so," she said.

I gave Dr. Mortimer a hug goodbye, holding on a little longer than usual.

I didn't know what my story was. I started the dinner happy and somehow I ended up sad.

I loved Jesse more than ever. I loved him across life and death and the murkiness between our worlds. I knew that we belonged together.

But I wasn't sure if I would ever see him again.

Chapter 9

I was always a little lost on Saturdays. I never worked on the weekends and there was no soccer either. Kate was usually out, at the newspaper or with Colin, and the house was quiet and empty.

I decided to start running in the park where Jesse and I used to hang out. I didn't want it to make me sad or anything, but I figured I could work on my speed for soccer and look for him at the same time.

It was a nice afternoon and not too crowded. The running path I was on looped around the park before disappearing into the forest and coming back out at the swings. It was half a mile and I planned on starting with four laps.

I had put together a good running playlist on my iPod and turned up the volume. Wolfmother pulsated through my ears as I picked up speed. I ran past some kids, past the "fitness boot camp" group that was working out with weights on the grass, past the dogs playing in their gated area. I scanned the basketball courts, watching some boys in the middle of an intense game.

I flashed back to when Jesse and I went to a Portland Trail Blazers game with his dad. We were just kids then and had nosebleed seats and ate too many hot dogs. But it was fun and Jesse talked about it for weeks after.

"You'll be coming to all my games, right?"

I laughed. We were still in elementary school and he had just started playing basketball in the afterschool sports program. He was kind of short back then, too.

"Come on, Abby. I'm talking about when I sign my contract. Of course, I'll be on the Spurs so you'll have to move to San Antonio. But I'll buy you some cowboy boots if you come along with me."

I smiled.

"I'll need a swimming pool too," I said.

"Deal," he said.

It felt good to be able to run. Sometimes it was hard to believe that a little more than a year ago I had trouble just walking to the Jeep. There were so many days that I was sure that I would never be able to run or play soccer again.

And now I was doing both.

I started thinking about my plans for September, when the river guide job was done. Kate said I could probably work part-time over at the newspaper on the features desk as an assistant. She had a friend who was the editor of that section and had offered me a position if I wanted it. I would be in charge of the calendar section, checking dates of events and making sure everything was correct. It would be a tedious desk job, but I felt I could do it if it came down to it.

Ty and a few others taught skiing up at the mountain and asked if that was something I would be interested in. But I knew I wasn't ready for the slopes yet. My balance wasn't there, I could tell. I really liked their lifestyle though, going from one fun job to another, depending on the season.

I thought about the guides and how much they were always smiling. They really loved what they did. They were outdoors and interacting with people and even though they didn't make much money, they were the happiest people I'd ever been around.

That's what I wanted. I wanted to find that. Something I loved doing so it didn't even feel like I was working. I was pretty sure that the newspaper job wasn't going to be like that.

But I didn't really know what I liked to do. I liked soccer and running and river rafting, but I couldn't think of any sort of career that would involve those things. I mostly knew what I didn't want to do. I didn't want to be inside at a cubicle, and I for sure didn't want to be in a classroom.

I looked up ahead at the cluster of trees I was about to run through. It was dark in the forest, covered in thick shadows. Weak sunlight cascaded through the branches up above. The shade felt good though. I was hot and working up a good sweat.

I looked up ahead and stopped.

She stood in the distance just off the path, lingering in the trees, staring at me with those razor sharp eyes.

Chills shot through my body. Again.

I pulled out my ear buds, trying to catch my breath but never taking my eyes off her. Her white dress blew behind her. She looked exactly the same as she had that day on the river, her wet hair matted down around her head and gown, that same dead expression. Her face was stark white with large, dark circles surrounding those piercing eyes.

She stood there, waiting. Waiting for me.

A gust of cold air slammed into me. The hairs on the back of my neck stood up. She kept staring, refusing to let go of my eyes.

I shivered as I backed away slowly before turning around and taking off back to the park. I ran as fast as I could, back to the sun, back to the people playing on the grass. Back to normal. I didn't stop until I got to the Jeep, didn't look back until I was inside with the doors locked.

She hadn't followed me, but I needed to get away. I quickly started the car and drove out of the parking lot.

With my heart still thundering in my chest and my body shaking, I weaved down the street and headed home.

That was twice now. Twice that I'd seen her.

No other ghost in the past year had done what she was doing.

She was stalking me.

Chapter 10

I was glad the house was still empty when I pulled up.

I was shaking as I stood in the shower, letting hot water rain down on me. I hoped it would wash away the dark feeling. There was something awful about that ghost, something horrifying.

She carried with her the same darkness I used to feel. That darkness from the lake.

I stayed under the water for a long time. When I finally came out, the bathroom was like a sauna with dense steam hanging thick in the air. I wrapped myself in towels and a robe and headed over to my computer.

I had told Kate about those others that I had seen on the streets and I would tell her about this one too. Just not yet. I didn't want her to worry. Also, if she knew I'd seen the ghost on the river she'd want me to quit my job.

For now, I needed Claire's opinion.

I had found Claire on the internet six months ago when I wasn't getting anywhere on my own in my search for Jesse. I had a sinking feeling that he was getting farther and farther away from me and I needed to know what had happened to him. If he was okay. I knew he wouldn't leave me if he had a choice. I wanted to know whether he was gone for good or if he still was out there. Needing me.

I felt kind of stupid looking for a medium online. There were thousands of them, all willing to help in exchange for a credit card number. But I wasn't a fool. I knew that most of them were fakes. Most of the sites I visited left me with a bad feeling, and I knew they were taking advantage of sad, desperate people. So I kept looking, hoping to find one real one who could help me. One was all I needed.

It had taken a few weeks to find her. But when I did, it felt right.

Claire was a single mom who lived in London and who always had "the gift" of seeing spirits and dead people, according to her website. I didn't know what it was about her, maybe just a feeling. But she was the only one I contacted.

I knew that Kate and Dr. Mortimer and Dr. Krowe would say that it was just proof that I still hadn't accepted Jesse's death and that I needed more therapy. So I didn't tell anyone about what I was doing.

I wrote to her to see if she could help me. And when I told her that I had seen and talked to Jesse for months after he died, she believed me. She told me it happened like that sometimes, that sometimes spirits stayed around because they weren't ready to let go.

We never spoke on the phone, only through email or instant message. She said she wanted to help because I had an "interesting energy" and that she would like to work with me. She never did end up charging me for anything either.

I didn't know what she was talking about. But I was excited. Maybe it had something to do with what Jesse had told me at the lake, that we were *in betweeners*. I didn't really care about any of that though. I just wanted to find Jesse.

But Claire couldn't find Jesse either. She was asking her guides for help and calling out to him across the frozen

62

land of the dead, as she put it. She told me not to give up hope, that there was still time and that maybe there was a reason he hadn't been in contact with me.

But she also said something else.

Claire warned me to prepare myself. Jesse may have moved on.

I took the towel off my wet head and entered her site. She always had a new message on her page. Today's message was about how we were all eternal beings and we would one day be reunited with our loved ones who had died.

I typed out a quick note telling her about my encounters with the ghost and what she looked like. I also wrote about how she scared me and asked how I could get her to leave me alone.

I didn't know how long it would take for Claire to write back. She was usually pretty fast, but she did have a full time job and two little kids. And then there was the time difference between Oregon and England.

I closed my laptop and sat back, checking the clock. I had a few hours before the concert. I yawned and realized I was exhausted. I dried my hair and got into bed, falling fast into a deep sleep.

Chapter 11

By the time I left for the concert, I felt better. I hadn't heard back from Claire, but that was okay. That dark feeling that had followed me home from the park was gone and I was looking forward to getting outside and being with people.

Ty was waiting by Red Robin for me. It was funny to see him in his regular clothes because they were exactly the same as his guide clothes. River sandals, a T-shirt, and shorts. The only change was his hair. It seemed fluffier or something.

"Hi," he said, smiling. "Good to see you. You look really nice."

I was dressed casually, but I had on capris and a tank top with dressier shoes. I put on a little mascara and lip gloss, so I must have looked a little different.

"Good to see you too," I said.

Swarms of people passed us carrying bags and blankets, heading to the amphitheater.

"Please, allow me," Ty said, wrapping his arm around the strap of my beach chair.

"Thanks."

We followed the crowd and headed to the concert. I loved this venue. It was a great place to listen to music. There was a large, grassy area with a big stage up front.

I had seen Lyle Lovett here with Kate a few years back and Death Cab for Cutie with my high school soccer team before my accident.

We walked through the gates and handed over our tickets. The river slid by on the right. There were already two canoes and a few kayakers anchored to the little sand island in the middle, waiting to hear the concert for free.

Most of the lawn was already filled up with people and blankets and chairs.

"Amber got us a spot up front," Ty said. "She got here hours ago."

I nodded. I had that fluttery nervous feeling but couldn't figure out why. It wasn't the same feeling I had with the ghost. It was something else. Then it came to me. Ty had asked me out to dinner a while ago, and I had never answered. With everything that was going on, I had forgotten.

"Want some ice cream?" he asked. "My treat."

"Yeah, that would be great," I said.

He nodded and got in line. When he returned, he held up an ice cream sandwich and a drumstick.

"Pick your poison."

"I'll take the sandwich."

We stood by the fence, eating, staring up at the stage. A few roadies were setting up for the opening act and testing the sound equipment.

"So what did you do today, Abby Craig?" Ty said. "Something exhilarating, I hope."

I finished chewing and thought about the ghost. It was exhilarating, but probably not in the way he meant.

"Not too much," I said. "Went for a run. Had a nap. You?"

"Smith Rock. I'm learning how to rock climb."

"Wow," I said. "That sounds fun."

"Yeah, I've always wanted to do it. It's beautiful out there. Have you been?"

I nodded my head.

Smith Rock was about 30 miles northeast of Bend and had amazing sheer cliffs, rock walls, and deep river canyons. It was a popular area with climbers from all over the country. There were hiking trails as well, along the Crooked River. Kate and I had gone with Mom when we were kids.

"Yeah, I've been once, but it was a long time ago. We did the hike to the top. I remember my legs burning because it was so steep. We saw a rattlesnake, too."

"I love it out there," he said.

We tossed out the wrappers.

"Let's go find the gang," he said.

I tried to summon my courage. I didn't want to just not say anything. I didn't want to hurt his feelings.

"Hey, Ty, about that dinner," I said, sounding a little too rehearsed.

He paused for a moment looking at the ground before meeting my eyes.

"I was wondering if you'd forgotten. You know, that I asked. Then I thought maybe you were still mad at me about the river thing, when I threw you in."

"Oh, no, it's nothing like that," I said. "I've just been busy lately. And I had to think about it."

That sounded stupid. I felt my cheeks getting prickly hot, no doubt turning six shades of red. This was ridiculous. My heart was fluttering like hummingbird wings, quivering strangely in my chest. I kept going, though. I had to explain things to him.

"It's just, well, I was involved with someone for a long time. A real long time. And now I'm not, but I still really care for him. I guess it feels a little too soon. But I wanted

66

you to know, if it wasn't for that, I'd love to go to dinner with you. I mean, I think you're great. Really."

I looked away for a moment, breathing in the soft evening air and trying to relax. Ty smiled, his bright energy dancing around like fireflies captured in a jar.

"Hey, I understand."

We started walking over toward the blankets to get our seats.

"But, you know, I was just thinking it would be a dinner. Just as friends, I mean. Can't we do that?"

We walked up the grassy aisle and over toward our group.

"At least think about it," he said. "And if you decide to come out with me, I promise to leave the engagement ring at home."

He laughed and I punched him lightly in the arm.

"Hey, there they are," Amber yelled when she saw us.

It was a great spot on the lawn, just a few rows back from the stage. Everyone was already there, plus a few others I didn't recognize, sitting on blankets and beach chairs among bottles of wine. Amber did some quick introductions.

Ty set up our chairs and I sat down, waiting for my heartbeat to settle back into a normal rhythm and for the music to take me away.

Chapter 12

I slid off my sandals and let my bare feet sink into the grass. The opening band took the stage and hammered out their set as a few gray-haired adults and little kids danced up in the open areas in the front. The sun was still pretty high in the sky, but not for long. I was glad I brought a hoodie. I knew that once the sun fell behind Mt. Bachelor, the temperature would drop substantially.

As I sat looking around, I thought how weird it was. Somehow being out in big, noisy crowds comforted me in a way. I didn't like to get too close to people, but for some reason I found it soothing to sit anonymously in large groups. I liked being around happy strangers.

"Hey, Ty. Deschutes is on tap, if you want it," Amber said. "I know you're not a wine guy. It's up over there at the booth."

"Awesome!" he said, standing up. "Be right back."

He left and I sat listening to the music while Amber told a story about one of her rafting groups.

"Abby, you doing okay?" she asked when she finished. "You seem quiet."

I didn't know Amber very well and she didn't really know me. She was talkative and outgoing. I was usually quiet and it seemed to make her uncomfortable. She was always asking me if I was okay. I supposed it would take her a little while to get used to me.

"Oh, everything's really good. Just enjoying the music."

Ty returned and sat down with a plastic cup of beer.

"Man, this is pure liquid gold. This pale ale rocks! It's my favorite. That's why I moved here, you know."

"What?" I said.

"Yep. I drank it back in Montana, so when I was looking for a new place to move to, I checked out Bend, Oregon, the home of Deschutes Brewery. And the rest is history."

"That's the craziest story I've ever heard," Amber said. "Moving somewhere 'cause you love their beer."

"I've heard crazier," Jake said. "I came here for a girl."

Ty smiled, his energy bright as he looked over at me.

"Yeah, but it's true. That beer is the best," Amber said. "You should go get a job at the plant, Ty. Complete your fantasy."

Everybody laughed. I smiled while I scanned the crowd.

"Nature calls," I said. "I'll be back."

"Want me to go with you?" Ty asked.

"No, but thanks. I got it. Drink your gold."

I walked around the blankets and got to the main path that led to the bathrooms. Nature didn't really call, but I needed a chance to think. That white energy moving rapidly around Ty made me nervous. I had seen it before, around Kate and Dr. Mortimer.

I headed over to the back and looked at the T-shirts for sale. Then I looked around for a moment. Just in case. There were a lot of tall guys in baseball caps, but none of them were Jesse.

As I walked back, I caught sight of Jack Martin in the beer line. I walked up and said hello.

"Hey, AC. What are you doing here?"

He seemed a little off, not quite himself. Of course, he wasn't playing soccer. It was hard to imagine Jack doing anything else.

"Hey, I almost didn't recognize you without a jersey on," I said.

His energy was gray and wobbly. He ordered his beer and walked with me. I pointed out where we were sitting.

"We're all the way at the back," he said.

"Are you with some of the team?" I asked.

I figured I should go say hello. It was the summer of making friends, I reminded myself.

"Oh, no," Jack said. "I wish. I'm with my cousin. He's visiting from back East and he's driving me insane. Seriously insane."

I smiled. That explained his mood.

"I don't even like this singer," he said, sipping from his cup. "But I'm trying to fill up the hours."

I nodded.

"Okay then, see you Tuesday at the game," I said. "Hang in there."

He smiled and downed more of his beer.

"This should help."

At about eight Ray LaMontagne took the stage, thanking the cheering fans for coming out and listening to him play. He started the set with *Hold You in My Arms*, one of my favorite songs.

It was a good night.

Chapter 13

After the concert, we all hung out for a little while longer, finding some seats in the courtyard in between restaurants on the other side of the river. Everybody started talking about where they were from. I was surprised that none of them were from Bend, or even Oregon for that matter. Amber was from Washington, Jake and Desmond from California, and Dylan was from Idaho. And then there was Ty, who was born and raised in Montana.

After about an hour, we meandered over to the parking lot. They were all going on to the clubs downtown. I said goodbye. Ty walked me to the Jeep.

"See you Monday," he said.

"Yeah, see ya. Have fun tonight."

"Oh, I'm heading home. It was a long day climbing and I'm beat," he said, smiling as he backed away.

"Okay. Get some good sleep then."

I couldn't stop thinking about Ty as I drove. Maybe I needed to take the advice I'd given to Kate. Maybe going out to dinner with him just wasn't the biggest deal I was making it out to be. Ty was a friend and it was nice. I really missed having a good friend.

The house was dark and empty. Kate wasn't home yet and I had again forgotten to leave some lights on. I hated walking into a dark house. It always gave me the creeps.

After I opened the door and entered the alarm code, I ran from room to room turning on all the lights.

I went to my computer and logged on, hoping Claire had written back. As I waited for the computer to start, I did the math. It must be too soon. It was only eight in the morning over in London now. She probably hadn't even had a chance to read my email.

But I saw a message from her in my inbox and opened it.

Abby,
I think this spirit needs your help. I think she's a strong spirit and won't be going away anytime soon. There is something she needs, something you can help her with.
Maybe if you help her, she can help you. With finding Jesse, I mean.
Cheers,
Claire

I closed the computer, leaned back in the chair, and suddenly felt like crying.

I had been such an idiot.

Why hadn't I thought of this sooner?

The ghost. Maybe Jesse had sent her.

Chapter 14

Things were different now. I was the one who would be stalking her, finding out what she wanted. And what she knew.

The next morning I drove back over to the park and walked down the path that led into the forest.

I had made a mistake. In my desperation and fear maybe I had ruined my chances at seeing Jesse again. Maybe Jesse needed me. Maybe the ghost was trying to tell me something about him. Why had I acted like such frightened fool?

I was so busy trying to ignore her that I had stopped thinking clearly.

But not anymore. I would push down my fear and bring up my courage. I would find her again, see what she wanted, and find Jesse.

I was alone again on the path as I headed into the shadows of the forest. I walked slowly, looking behind the trees and shrubs. I came to the spot where I saw her when I was running, but she wasn't there.

"I'm here," I said out loud. "I'm ready to talk now."

But nothing answered back. It was dead quiet.

I stayed for over an hour, walking around and thinking. Two runners ran by and then a group of women from the boot camp thundered through. But no ghost.

I wasn't discouraged though. I had a pretty good idea where I could find her.

Chapter 15

It was on the third run through the rapids when I saw her. Across the river from the take-out, pacing back and forth in white, high up on the lava rock cliff. I watched her out of the corner of my eye as we said goodbye to the tourists.

I had been looking for her all day and had a strong, stomach-on-the-floor feeling that I would find her on the river. She was in the same area where I had first seen her, across from where Ty had thrown me in the water. But I wouldn't be able to get to her until after work. I could only hope that she would wait.

As we headed back up river for the final run, I asked Ty if there was a road on the other side.

"Nope," he said. "No access. There's not even a trail over there. Why?"

"Oh, I'm rock collecting," I said. "Really wanted to add some of that ancient lava to round out my collection."

I knew that sounded dumb, but it was all that came to me.

"I can take you over when we're through later. If it's just for a few minutes."

"That would be great."

I had six women from Nevada in my last group. They were nice enough, but didn't seem to be too into the river trip. They were attending some conference in Bend all week and talked about that among themselves in between the rapids. I didn't mind. It gave me time to figure out what I would say to the ghost. The tourists were still talking about one of the presenters as they got out of the boat and walked back to the bus. I didn't get a tip.

After their bus pulled out of the lot, we started loading up to go home. Ty walked up to me.

"What if I take you over now and come back for you in 15 minutes?"

"Great. Thanks, Ty. I really appreciate it."

"Let me go tell the others what we're doing. I'll be right back."

I glanced back up at the cliff. She was still there.

As Ty paddled us across, I worked on my courage. He steered the raft up against the rocks, back paddling to hold us steady. I jumped up onto the small landing.

"Okay, see you in fifteen. But being that I'll be doing all your packing-up work this afternoon, I think you owe me a dinner."

"You're on," I said.

I looked up. Except for the sharp edges of the black rocks, the climb wasn't too bad. When I got to the top, a cold breeze blew into me, drying the nervous sweat that was dripping down my face. Those stark eyes locked into mine immediately. I rubbed my palms together and took deep breaths as I walked up to her, slowly, step by step. My heart was pounding in my ears, but I reminded myself I was doing this for Jesse. Jesse might need me.

A dark energy swirled in and around her as she glared. She was angry.

I took a step closer, forcing my shaking legs to move. I could see her better now. She was older than me, maybe about Kate's age. Her long, black hair was wet and clinging to her face and dress. There were gashes on her arms and legs.

Chills shot through my body as I looked at her and tried to find the words I had been rehearsing in my head.

"Ddd... ddd... ddd..." I stuttered. My stomach was woozy and I wasn't sure if my knees would hold me up much longer. "Did Jesse send you?"

She didn't say anything, but started moving toward me. I took a step back, but then forced myself to stay put, planting my feet. Tears streamed down my cheeks.

She put an icy hand on my face as she glared at me. I couldn't breathe, couldn't get any oxygen. I was captured by that blackness that surrounded her. I closed my eyes, preparing to be thrown off the rocks, back into the deep, dark waters below.

But she didn't push me.

Her hand was frosty on my face, but it was gentle as it turned my head toward the river. I opened my eyes and tried to breathe as she pointed to the water, to the spot where I'd first seen her.

Before vanishing, she put her hand on her chest. And then she was gone.

Chapter 16

I decided to tell Kate about the ghost. I entered the code for the alarm after I unlocked the door. I would tell her everything after dinner. I needed her help.

I was pretty sure I understood what the ghost was saying, that her body was down at the bottom of the Deschutes River. I didn't know what she wanted, but I had to start by finding out who she was and what had happened to her.

I emailed an update to Claire and walked out to the kitchen. I was making enchiladas for dinner. I saw a cooking show earlier in the week and had figured I would give it a try. I set up my laptop on the counter, found the saved recipe, and began working on the chicken.

In about an hour, I had everything ready to put it all together. I heated the tortillas individually in a frying pan before soaking them in the sauce I had made and then filled them with the chicken mixture, rolling them up and grating cheddar cheese over the top.

I sighed as I waited. I was nervous about telling Kate and was trying to think of a way to tell her that wouldn't make her upset. She wouldn't like that I saw a ghost on the river, but I couldn't leave out the river setting because it was an important part of her story.

I heard the door open and shouted out a hello. Kate walked in and patted my shoulder, asking about dinner and flinging her shoes across the floor.

By the time she returned in sweats, I had plated our dinner adding avocado and sour cream, lit a candle, and poured her a Corona. We sat eating at the dining room table.

"Amazing, hit me again," Kate said, holding out her empty plate. "You have a real talent."

I smiled.

"Thanks," I said, shrugging.

We asked each other about our days. I was vague, but she didn't seem to notice. She was in a happy mood, which was unusual lately.

"It goes to the jury tomorrow and I don't think it will take them long to decide," she said.

"Good," I said.

"I stopped by the police station to say hello to some old friends. I miss them."

"I bet they were happy to see you."

"They were. It was really nice."

After dinner we headed over to the TV, throwing ourselves like pillows on the sofa. We watched a little of the local news before Kate flipped it to Cold Case Files.

"Hey, Colin might stop by later. He's bringing a documentary on the South during the Civil Rights Movement. You can watch with us if you want."

"Oh, sure," I said.

We watched the show for a few minutes.

"Hey, Kate," I finally said.

"Hmmm."

"I wanted to talk to you about something. Is it a good time?"

She shot a quick, intense look over to me. I knew that she was thinking about Nathaniel.

79

"No, nothing about *him*. I promise. It's something else."

She seemed relieved and muted the TV.

"What's up?"

"This is going to sound weird, I know. But. Well. I've been seeing this ghost and need your help."

"A ghost?" she repeated.

"Yeah."

I had told Kate about Jesse, and knew she was never too sure about whether I had seen him or invented him. But she hadn't totally written it off. She knew my visions about Nathaniel had been real and was open to the possibility that I saw ghosts too.

"So where did you see it?" she asked.

Her eyes were wide and serious.

I told her all about it, including how I saw her on the river. I said that the ghost seemed to need something, and that I wasn't able to ignore her anymore.

"What do you mean, she needs something?"

I could tell that it made her angry.

"What right does she have to want anything from you? Jeez, you need to move on from all this, you know? You've paid your dues and then some. Don't get involved."

I took a deep breath. This was harder than I thought it was going to be.

"I can't not get involved," I said. "I don't have a choice."

I wasn't going to mention how I thought the ghost might help me find Jesse.

"Not have a choice? What does that mean? Are you in danger?"

"No, it's nothing like that. I promise, I'm safe. I'm sure of it."

I wasn't really sure, but I sounded confident and I could see that Kate relaxed a little. She threw her head back on the cushion and exhaled slowly.

"And you're absolutely sure it has nothing to do with his brother? How can you know?"

I did actually know, but didn't know how to explain it.

"I'm positive. This isn't like that. Not at all. I've been seeing ghosts this past year. I've told you about them. They're out walking around. I know it sounds nuts, but you wanted me to tell you about these things, and that's what I'm doing."

What I was saying was true, although I also needed more from Kate than just an ear.

"This ghost has come to me and needs help. And I'm going to help her."

"I don't like this part of your life, Abby," she said, crossing her arms. "It scares me and brings up all that stuff again. Can't you just walk away and let her find someone else?"

We sat watching the television for a while. The investigators were at the lab doing new DNA tests.

"Okay," Kate said. "Tell me what she said. Tell me what the ghost wants."

I told her that she was at the bottom of the river and needed my help finding her body.

"Oh, great. Perfect," Kate said. "A drowning."

"Drowning?" I said. "Wow. That's funny but I never even thought of that."

Kate looked at me strangely.

"Yeah, it's hilarious," she said. "What else would it be?"

"I don't know. But it's something more. She didn't speak to me, she just pointed to the river. But I got this dark feeling about it. I don't think she drowned. I'm pretty sure it was something else."

I knew that would pique Kate's interest a little. She was a natural detective and loved solving mysteries.

"So, you think she was murdered? Is that what you're thinking?"

As she said the word *murdered*, I knew.

"Yeah, I think that's exactly what happened."

"If that's the case, then it must be unsolved, right? If her body hasn't been found, if she's still in the river, then she must be listed as a missing person."

"That makes sense," I said.

Kate was quiet for a moment.

"I guess I can dig up the unsolved missing person files for you. I'll bring them home this week. If you can identify her, we can go from there. How long do you think it's been? Any idea?"

"I'm not really sure," I said.

"Well, I know there have only been a few people here in Bend who have been reported missing these past few years. And a few have been found. Let's see. There was one young guy who got lost up in the mountains, and of course there was that woman who disappeared last year. So maybe I should go back 10 years or so. I'll see what I can find out."

"That would be great."

"So how old do you think she is?"

"She's a little older than you," I said. "Long black hair, medium height, thin. She's dressed in white."

"Aren't all ghosts dressed in white?"

"I guess."

But I was thinking of Jesse. Jesse was always dressed in his street clothes.

Kate sighed.

"Of course I'll help you. You know that. I'm here for you. But I need one thing from you."

I braced. I didn't want her to ask me to quit my river guide job.

"You have to promise me that you won't get so involved in all this," she said, sitting up a little. "I'm serious. Do what you think you need to do for this ghost and move on. You have a lot of good things going on in your life now. You've come back all the way and you're doing great. You're the happiest I've seen you since…"

She suddenly stopped talking and looked away.

"The happiest since that horrible accident. You can't let this business pull you back down. We can't go there again no matter who needs your help. You have to promise me that before I'll help you."

"I promise," I said.

I knew this was all hard for her. I knew she didn't want to see me that way ever again.

"If she's down in the river, let's find her and bring her up. But that'll be it. Promise?"

"Promise."

Kate was right. I had worked too hard to escape from the darkness of that lake. She was looking after me and I appreciated it.

"Good. Okay, if the verdict in the trial is early, I'll bring home what I can get tomorrow afternoon."

"Sounds great," I said.

"Hey, as long as we're having an open, honest discussion, I might as well show you what I bought."

She stood up abruptly and went toward her bedroom. I already knew what she was going to show me because I had found it last week. I wasn't being snoopy or anything, but came across it when I was looking for eye drops in her nightstand.

She returned carrying a little wooden box. She put it on the coffee table, sat on the sofa, and opened it slowly.

It sat in velvet. Black, shiny, and deadly.

"I know I should have told you when I first got it," she said, picking up the gun like a professional and pointing it out in front of us. "But I didn't want to upset you. I know you're not a big fan of guns. I got it to protect us. And I have to admit that since I bought it, I sleep a lot better at night."

I nodded.

"I don't mind. Especially if it makes you feel better."

She looked at me with intense eyes.

"*He* said he'd come back for you," she said. "I'm not letting that happen."

I couldn't argue with that. It was exactly what Nathaniel said before he escaped. It helped that Dr. Mortimer told us that he wasn't in the country anymore, but it would be foolish to let our guard down. It wasn't over, and we both knew that.

"Here," she said, handing me the gun. "Go ahead and hold it. It's not loaded."

I hadn't ever seen a real one before in my life. I took it from Kate and held it out in front of me. It was heavier than I thought.

"Pow," she whispered.

Holding it in my hands made me a little sad. I thought about how we had changed. This wasn't who we were, or at least who we used to be. And I didn't like that we were different because of him.

"It's heavy."

"Yep. It has a lot of power. One of the officers helped me pick it out."

I nodded.

Holding the gun also made me realize how scared Kate was. While I was busy rafting down the river and making friends, she had obviously been thinking about Nathaniel.

84

"Abby, I want you to come with me to the shooting range. I've been a few times and I want you to come too."

I really didn't want to learn how to use a gun. But I would for her.

"Sure. Just tell me when and where and I'll be there," I said, handing it back to her.

Kate smiled as she placed it carefully back in the box.

"I keep it in my nightstand, along with a box of cartridges. I've also hidden some other boxes in the cupboard next to the light bulbs and in your room next to your old games in the closet."

I nodded. Wow. She really was serious.

"I don't want to scare you, but you know what he is capable of and we need to be ready. Nothing is going to happen to you. I promise you that."

I tried to smile. She got up, picked up the small box, and walked back to her bedroom.

She was right, but it didn't feel good. I watched the show until she returned.

"I want you to know that I haven't forgotten about him," she said.

"I know that. Probably why you put in the alarm system, right?"

"Yep," she said. "It's also why I almost bought a German Shepherd last month. Sometimes I wonder if we should just get the hell out of here and go into hiding."

She sat down and finished the last of her beer.

"But the best solution is to get him. He's just human, you know. Visions or no visions, a bullet through his brain will stop his insanity instantly."

That didn't sound like Kate at all. It was shocking that she would say that, that killing Nathaniel was the best solution.

"Sorry," she said, looking at my expression.

"Or we could put him in jail, right?"

"Of course. Sure. Ideally. But it's not so easy with the police messing up. We'd have to get some sort of evidence on him. They totally blew the entire case and he got away with murder."

"Just let me know when you want to go," I said.

I wanted to change the subject.

"Good," she said. "And I'll bring home those files for you, hopefully tomorrow."

The show was ending. The detectives nailed the husband for murdering his wife after 20 years.

"See," Kate said. "Justice may not always be swift, but it happens. Especially if I have any say in it."

Chapter 17

I found myself wishing that the day would go by faster. I didn't usually have those thoughts. I was never bored on the river. But since the first run down, I couldn't stop thinking about the files and was hoping Kate could get them to me tonight.

The ghost wasn't on the river. I looked for her, but she wasn't there. I hoped she knew I was trying to help.

At the end of the day we loaded up the bus and headed back to the office. I sat next to Ty as we bounced along the dirt road before making it to the highway.

We signed out and stepped back outside into the heat. It had been a scorching day and even though it was after five, it was hotter than ever.

"So, when are we going?" Ty asked.

I was ready this time and wasn't even nervous. In fact, I was prepared to bring it up if he didn't.

"How about Friday?" I said.

"Great," he said, smiling. He pulled down his sunglasses, hiding his happy eyes.

"I was thinking too, that maybe after an early dinner, we could hike up Pilot Butte," I said. "If you want. It's got great views of the mountains."

Pilot Butte was an ancient cinder cone that sat in the middle of town, with both a road and a primitive hiking trail leading up to the top. The July 4th firework show took place at the summit every year. It was a mile hike and had an epic view of Bend, the nearby badlands, and all the surrounding mountains.

"I'd love to. I haven't been up there," he said. "Sounds fun."

We said goodbye in the lot and I drove home, battling that guilty feeling that floated around my insides now whenever I thought about Ty. He was just a friend, I told myself.

I was disappointed that Kate's Subaru wasn't in the driveway. But as I checked my messages in the car, I got excited. There was one from her and she said that she had collected all the missing person files in the last ten years from Bend PD and had brought them home at lunch. They were on the kitchen table.

"But don't get your hopes up," she said as I turned the key in the lock. "I only pulled ones that fit her description. There aren't too many."

I rushed inside and ran over to the kitchen.

There were only three files on the table. I was discouraged, but as I picked them up, I reminded myself that I only needed one.

I scanned through them, going directly to the pictures.

She wasn't there.

I sighed and got a bottle of water from the fridge and made my way back over to the missing women.

The files had such a sad, heavy energy to them. I flipped through the first one, noting the name and the dates, and then through the other two.

One woman had disappeared leaving work late one night. Her family was offering a big reward for any information. I stared at her picture for a long time. She was the right age, but had short hair and an angular face. The next file was about a woman who was in her 30's and lived in Ohio, but was last seen in Bend. And finally, there was a woman who went out into the wilderness on a hike by herself, but never returned.

My heart sank. Not just for the ghost I was trying to find, but for these women who must have had loved ones looking for them. It made me think of my own search for Jesse, reminding me that the world was full of lost sheep and lost love. Maybe me losing Jesse wasn't really so unique after all.

It didn't make any sense that she wasn't in the files. Someone must have reported her missing. Maybe the time period was all wrong. Maybe we needed to go back farther, like 20 years or more.

I went to my room, opened my laptop, and checked my email. Claire had written early in the morning telling me to keep trying and not give up. That was weird. I wondered if she sensed that it wouldn't be so easy finding out about the ghost.

"Keep helping her, Abby. She probably has a family out there who is missing her terribly."

My heart sank when I read that. That dark energy swirling around her wasn't evil. She wasn't mean or dangerous; she was just lost. Her family probably had no idea what had happened to her. She had just vanished from their lives forever.

No wonder she was so angry.

I closed the computer.

"We'll find you," I said out loud, hoping she could hear me. "I promise."

Chapter 18

I was sleeping by the time Kate returned and she was gone when I woke up. She left a note telling me to call her when I got up. She was doing the big wrap up on the trial and would be at her desk at *The Bugler* all day.

"Hey, Abby," she said, picking up her phone on the first ring.

I could tell she was in a hurry. I got to the point.

"She's not in any of these files," I said.

"Yeah, I had that feeling," she said. "I'll go back farther, if you want."

"Okay. I don't think it was that long ago, though."

Kate was quiet for a moment.

"Okay. Let me think some more on this. I'm on deadline for the web edition of a story, but we'll talk later. Hey, can you go to the range tonight? I made us a reservation. I knew it wasn't a soccer night for you."

"Sure," I said.

"Great. I'll be home a little early."

I thanked her and clicked off. Kate was good at her job. She would come up with something.

I got ready for work and headed to the river, hoping that the angry ghost of the missing woman had some patience.

Chapter 19

I didn't really want to go, but I had promised. We had an early quick dinner and I cleaned up.

"Should I wear anything special?"

"You're fine as is," Kate said. "Let's get going."

We drove out of town and into the desert. Kate rolled down the windows and the hot summer air blew our hair around, but it felt good.

"Nervous?" she asked, turning up Josh Ritter as he sang *Come and Find Me*.

"Come and find me, Jesse," I whispered under my breath.

"No," I said to Kate. "I think it's a good idea. Really. Hey, what did you think about that verdict? I saw it on the news."

"I was bummed, but not surprised. I know he's guilty, the bastard. He's too powerful. Guys like that seem to get away with everything."

Kate was quiet for a minute.

"But on to things we hopefully have more control over. I've given your case some thought and something came to me."

I liked the way she called it my case. And I was glad to hear she was thinking about those women. Maybe it was a good thing, in a way, her helping me.

"What if she isn't missing from Deschutes County? Maybe the murderer brought her here and dumped her body in the river."

"That's good," I said. "Real good."

"If that's what happened, it's both good and bad. I mean, she could be from anywhere. A different state, even thousands of miles away. She may be impossible to find."

"That's true," I said.

"And it would be nice to find out more about her before I go and ask the sheriff's department to search the river. If we knew who she was, we could talk to the family and have them put pressure on the department. That would be better than me telling them that my little sister has seen her ghost."

I smiled.

"Good point," I said.

"I can't expect too much help on this from Bend PD either," she said. "You know, with that whole business last year of me trying to get them to charge Dr. Mortimer's brother with murder. Even though it was true, I lost some credibility with that. We'll need something more for this."

"I think she has family," I said, remembering Claire's message.

"Tomorrow I'll search nearby counties and get you those files. Maybe we'll get lucky and stumble upon her. You never know."

"Sounds like a good plan."

"Here we go," she said, pulling into a dirt parking lot. It felt like we were in the middle of nowhere.

She reached over and grabbed the box from the glove compartment. I got to carry the rounds.

I followed her inside. We signed in, showed ID, and Kate gave them a credit card. The older man behind the counter handed us each some head earmuffs that were supposed to go over the ear plugs we brought. We walked through a thick, steel door and into the range.

It looked just like the ones that were in all those movies and shows on television, where the cops practiced their shooting. There were ten spots, separated by little walls, side by side. Large paper targets were hanging across from us, near the wall in the distance. I would be lucky if I hit anything.

"I'll go first, show you how it's done," she said as we put on the ear protection.

Kate loaded the gun, took off the safety, and fired a few rounds. After she finished, she pressed a button and the little paper man moved toward us.

"I need more practice, obviously," she said, looking at the target. But she had done pretty well.

She put a new target on the clip and pressed the button again.

"Your turn."

She showed me how to load it and how to stand. Then she handed me the gun.

"Be careful as you pull the trigger. When you fire it, make sure to brace."

I held the gun steady in my hands and pulled the trigger, missing the silhouette completely. I shot until the gun was empty.

We brought back the target. I hadn't hit any of the dark area.

"You'll get better," Kate said.

I was ready to go home, but we stayed and shot a few more rounds.

"We'll keep coming out here until we both can shoot the head off," she said. "With both eyes closed."

Chapter 20

Every day Kate brought home pictures of missing women for me to look through. She had been getting them faxed over to the newspaper from surrounding cities and counties and had contacted nearly all the small police and sheriff departments around the state. It was shocking to see how many people went missing every year, even from really small towns. But so far, we had had no luck. She wasn't there.

I was glad that Kate was interested in the case and willing to help out. The fire that had been sucked away during that long trial had returned, and she seemed back to her old self.

"We'll find her," she said. "We're on the right path. I can feel it."

"I hope so," I said.

It was a good week on the river. Most of the customers were friendly, although I had one older lady get upset because she lost her hat going down the first of the whitewater.

"That was an expensive one," she said. "Why didn't you remind me again to take it off before we went down?"

I glanced over to Ty, who had been listening and smiling.

When I got home, I found out that Dr. Mortimer was coming to the game that night. He had left a message saying he didn't have to go into the ER until later.

"I'll just meet you over at the field, Abby."

It was good to hear his voice. He sounded happy.

I called Kate to let her know. But she didn't pick up and I wondered if she was on her way to watch the game with Colin. I sent a text. Then another.

Dr. Mortimer was standing in the grass with his hands in his pockets. I walked up and said hello.

"Hey, Abby."

"Thanks for coming," I said.

"I'm thrilled to be out here. I've been trying to watch you play ever since the season started."

I smiled, feeling a little awkward. I still wasn't completely comfortable around him. It was better when Kate was with us.

"Wow. Here you are playing soccer again. It's just awesome."

"Yeah," I said. "And all because of you."

I meant that too.

It took me a while to realize that Dr. Mortimer was right about his brother. It was nonsense, pure mumbo jumbo, what Nathaniel had claimed, that I was some freakish research project of his and that he had been the one who had brought me back to life. And the more time that passed, the more I was grateful that Dr. Mortimer had been at the hospital that night and was able to save me. It was because of him, and only him, that I was on a soccer field again.

"Oh, no. It wasn't just me. We all played our parts. You especially. You're a hell of a fighter. Remember that."

I smiled again, a little embarrassed. I was so happy that he had come out to the game. He belonged in our family. It was just that nobody really knew where he fit in anymore.

I tossed down my water bottle and looked out at the field. Most of our team was already out there warming up. The ref walked over and began talking to the captains.

"Thought I would just give you a heads up," I said. I figured I might as well warn him too. "Kate sometimes comes out to my games when she can."

"Oh, that would be great," Dr. Mortimer said.

"Well, yeah, but Colin usually tags along."

"Okay." It didn't seem to bother him at all. "I would still love to see her."

I ran out and met Jack and the rest of the team on the field as someone kicked me the ball.

"Hey, AC," Jack said. "Ready for the game?"

"Oh, yeah. Thought about it all day," I said.

"So, who's that in your cheering section, now?" he asked, squinting in the lights, looking at Dr. Mortimer.

I told him it was a family friend and he passed me the ball again and I kicked it over to Bree.

We were in first place and had won all our games, but tonight we were facing a tough team. The ref blew the whistle and we kicked off. Within the first two minutes, we were down a goal.

"It's early, no worries," Bree said as we walked back to the middle of the field.

Right before the half, I was taken down by a jittery little guy with a thin mustache who had a reputation for slide tackling. He was fast and had caught up to me easily. Not exactly something I wanted Dr. Mortimer to see, but it was just part of the game. Especially out here. The ref gave him a yellow card and I took the free kick, passing it over to Jack. He took it in and scored a sweet goal to tie the game.

At the half, I scanned the sidelines. I was relieved to see that Dr. Mortimer was still standing by himself. Kate must have gotten my messages.

"Fantastic," Dr. Mortimer said, beaming.

I wasn't really fantastic, nothing like I used to be, but that was okay. It felt great just being able to play again.

In the second half, I had a chance to win it in the final minute, but their goalie stoned me. The game ended 1-1.

"Well, we're still in first place," Jack sighed, collecting his stuff and jamming it in his bag.

He was probably the most competitive person I had ever met and I imagined he hated tying as much as he hated losing.

"See you guys next week," he mumbled, walking away.

As I said goodbye to the rest of the team, I saw Kate pulling into the parking lot. She got out of the car and walked toward us. She was alone.

"Hey, Ben," she said.

She smiled.

"Hey, Kate. Boy, you just missed a great game. It was incredible watching Abby play."

"You always did say that she would play soccer again," she said. "You called it, even when she was having trouble just walking."

"She needed time to heal and healing is always on its own schedule. It's easy to get impatient."

He looked at me when he said that. It was true. I had been real impatient.

"She's really come a long way, hasn't she?" Kate said.

"She has," he said.

It felt like old times, the two of them talking about me. We stood under the bright stadium lights as the field emptied out. Ours was the last game of the night and almost everyone was gone or in the parking lot.

"I'm glad you came, Kate. I have some news, if you guys are up for it."

"Sure," she said. "What's up?"

"Here goes. The agency says that he's working in a refugee camp in Kenya. Now it's just a matter of physically finding him there."

Kate didn't say anything.

"That's good," I said.

"I still don't know what he would be doing there," Kate said. "But Abby's right. It's good to know where he is. So what's the next step?"

"I've asked the agency to start investigating the murders here in Bend. When they find something, we'll try and get those cases reopened and go from there."

Kate smiled finally, those bright waves moving above her head.

The lights above us suddenly turned off.

"Let's get over to the parking lot," she said. "I have a favor to ask, Ben. That's why I came tonight."

"Sure," Dr. Mortimer said, leading us toward the cars.

I looked up at the sliver of moon hanging low above the horizon and the stars peppering the black desert sky. It was a good feeling, hearing that they were close to finding Nathaniel. But I was also glad that he was so far away.

Chapter 21

Kate's favor seemed to make Dr. Mortimer happy. But it was still wrong the way she did it. It made me feel like a four-year-old.

"Could you come over to the house for a few days and stay with Abby?" Kate asked.

I was putting my bag into the backseat and hoped that I heard wrong. I slammed the trunk and joined them again.

"I have to go to Portland next week and don't want her staying alone."

"Of course," Dr. Mortimer said. "Just email me the dates. It would be my pleasure."

"Hey," I said. "Come on. I'm not a kid. I can stay by myself."

She looked over at me, her eyebrows high on her head. She seemed to realize what she had done.

"Oh, Abby. I'm sorry. I should have talked with you about it first. I didn't mean for it to sound like that. I would just feel better if someone were at the house while I was gone. That you weren't by yourself."

I rolled my eyes at her as I said goodbye.

"Thanks for coming out to the game, Dr. Mortimer," I said.

I got in the Jeep and drove home.

I was furious. Kate was out of line. There was no need to embarrass me like that in front of Dr. Mortimer and there was no need to bring in a babysitter for her 19-year-old sister. I tried to calm down as drove, but my anger just kept building. I threw myself, sweat and all, on the sofa and waited for her to get home.

Ten minutes later I heard the key in the door.

"Come on. I said I was sorry," she said. "I didn't mean anything by it. I wasn't thinking. It's just that I need to go to Portland and I don't want to leave you here by yourself and I knew you couldn't come with me because of your job. Come on. I'm sorry. Forgive me."

"I'm taking a shower," I said, getting up and walking away.

The water cooled off my anger somewhat. When I returned, Kate was watching TV.

"All right. I forgive you," I said, sitting down next to her.

She smiled and held out her hand and I shook it.

"Thanks, Abby. I wouldn't have liked that either. Sorry, again."

"But I don't need anybody coming over to the house and watching me. Seriously. That's just dumb."

"He's not watching you. I just didn't want anyone to notice you were here by yourself. I won't be able to go if I'm all freaked out about it. Could you just do it for me?"

"All right," I said after a long pause. "What's in Portland anyway?"

"The newspaper is sending me there to check on the background of a guy who was arrested last week for identity theft who used to live in Portland. He was using another name and had been serving as one of the county commissioners. Anyway, I figured I might as well look into the missing person files while I'm there."

"Oh, that would be good," I said.

"It works out too because there's a lot of them, so I wouldn't be able to get them all faxed over here to Bend anyway. It's just easier to be there and go through the files myself. Maybe I can get Erin to help me."

Erin was Kate's best friend. She used to work as a reporter at *The Bugler*, but last year she got a job in Portland at *The Oregonian*.

"That sounds good," I said.

"I'm going to go through what they have and take pictures of anyone fitting the description. Then I'll send those over to you. If we're lucky and you see her, maybe I can stay on in Portland and do some more investigating."

It started feeling real, like the ghost was connected to a person and a story.

"Sorry about getting so mad earlier," I said. "I hope I didn't hurt Dr. Mortimer's feelings."

"Are you kidding? He's super happy about coming over to help. You won't even see much of him with his schedule. It's just another car in the driveway and someone in and out of the house. That's all, Abby."

"Yeah, okay," I said. "But that was great news, too. About *him*, I mean. That they found him after all this time."

Kate nodded but didn't say anything for a few minutes. The glow from the television illuminated her face and I noticed she looked worried.

"Yes, it is. I'll feel better though when he's actually apprehended and facing charges and this whole nightmare is behind us."

"It's a step," I said. "And Dr. Mortimer is really trying."

Kate sighed.

"What's wrong?"

"I don't know. It's just a feeling I've been having lately," she said. "I can't tell if it's real or not."

She turned and looked at me, pulling her knees up and wrapping her arms around them.

"But you know how it is when things are going really well and then you wonder when the other shoe will drop? That's exactly how I feel. Nervous, or something. We have it good now, Abby. So I guess it's natural for me to think that something bad is going to happen."

"That's not true," I said. "Besides, haven't we paid our dues for a while? That's what you're always saying."

"I know, you're right. It's probably just nerves," she said. "It was real good news tonight about his brother. The first real news we've heard since he escaped."

"And it won't be bad having Dr. Mortimer here."

"I figured it was better than asking Colin to stay over," she said, smiling.

She stood up and yawned.

"I've got to get to bed. It's been a long day. Good night, Abby."

Chapter 22

It was cloudy on the river the next day and it started raining by midmorning, but it didn't seem to affect business. Our rafts were full on every run. The guides were in good moods and so were the tourists. I got a lot of good tips. At the end of the afternoon, the clouds broke apart and the sun came out. It turned out to be a beautiful day.

Although I looked on the river and up on the cliffs every time we pulled into the take-out, I didn't see her. I hoped she knew that I was trying to help. Sometimes, when I was standing alone on the bank and the customers had left, I would whisper in the wind that I was close to finding her. I hoped my words would cross between our worlds and offer some comfort.

Ty seemed especially happy all day and as we got on the bus, he sat next to me with a goofy grin splattered across his face.

"So where are we going?" he asked.

My stomach tightened a little but I smiled anyway.

"First an early dinner at a place I know you'll love. And then afterwards, we'll climb up to the top of Pilot Butte, if you're up for it."

"That's what I'm talking about," he said.

We signed out in the office and joked around with a few of the guides for a while before saying goodbye. I thought that maybe Ty would invite them along. Or actually, I wished he would. But he didn't.

"Okay, I'm ready," he said.

"Me too."

I drove us over to the Deschutes Brewery Pub. It was an easy choice since he loved their beer so much. We walked in and were seated by the window. It was still pretty early so it wasn't that crowded.

"Man, I love this place!" he said, looking around.

"You probably come here every night, but I couldn't think of a better spot," I said, fiddling with a paper napkin.

"You bet I do. I told them if my ski job doesn't work out that I'll apply here for a job, even if it's washing dishes."

"That would be perfect," I said. "I hear they pay in beer too."

Ty laughed. He looked good sitting in the restaurant, off the river, even with his hair matted down from wearing a hat all day. I liked being able to actually see his eyes. They were a light color, probably the lightest I'd ever seen.

We sat in an awkward silence for a minute. I was trying to think of something to say and he was unusually quiet.

"So, you like it in Bend?" I asked. "I mean, compared to Montana?"

He nodded quickly.

"Yeah, I really do. It's great. I miss my family, but I love living here. There's so much to do and the people are awesome too. Like you, Abby."

He looked at me for a minute as I smiled nervously. Now I felt super uncomfortable. I started laughing.

"Seriously, I mean it," he said. "You guys here are all so friendly."

I probably wouldn't completely agree with that, but I liked that Ty thought so.

"Do you have a big family?" I said.

"Yeah, it's pretty big. Four brothers and lots of uncles and aunts and about a million cousins. How about you? Do you have a big family?"

I shook my head.

"Well, there's my sister. And that's about it."

"Oh, wow."

"But we have a lot of friends."

It was really Kate who had lots of friends. I was working on it, but I didn't want to sound pathetic.

"You guys are lucky to have each other. And also to be living in such beauty."

He was right. Bend was really nice. With the rivers and mountains and fresh air and hot summers and snowy winters, I couldn't think of a better place to live. Most of the time, I really loved it here.

But there had been times when I felt differently. After my accident, I hated it. During my recovery there were a lot nights I stayed awake thinking about leaving, about going to a place where nobody had ever heard about me.

I hadn't felt like that lately, though. And that was a good feeling. It was starting to feel like I belonged here again.

We ordered and talked about the different groups of the day and how Amber had gotten stuck up against a rock on our third run for a few minutes.

"She's hooked herself on that same boulder three times so far," he said. "I don't get what she's doing. She's missing the channel. I'll have to run it with her once when we're by ourselves and see where she's going wrong."

"At least it's not the big rock in the middle of the river."

"Yeah, getting stuck on that one would flip you," he said. "Flip you for real."

I asked him if he had ever tipped a raft or had someone fall out in the water.

"Yeah, back in Montana a few years ago. It wasn't pretty, but nobody got seriously hurt. I had three people fall out and had to get them all back in. We were on a three-day trip. They were bruised and scared, but nothing else."

"Scary," I said.

"Just like we said in training, it happens sometimes. It's what you do when they are in the river that counts. It's all part of the adventure. Even here, on this little run we do all day. It's not a complete Disneyland ride. There are risks."

I nodded. I suddenly felt a little cold. It wasn't that I didn't know what Ty was saying, it was just that I didn't think about it most days.

"It's always good to be reminded though," he said. "And to never get too comfortable on the river. It's one of the most powerful forces of nature. Anything can happen out there."

Our food came. We started eating and I felt a little better.

"You really like what you do," I said. "River guide and ski instructor?"

"What can I say? It's a charmed life. I want to do this for as long as possible. So what are your plans for the fall?"

It was strange, but for the first time ever, I didn't tense up with that question. It felt like Ty was a good friend and it was normal for him to ask. Or maybe it was the casual way he had said it.

"I'm not really sure," I said.

I told him about all the things I didn't want to do. We both agreed that offices and suits shouldn't be in our futures.

We finished eating.

"Dinner was epic," Ty said.

"I knew you would like it," I said, settling back into the booth.

I wanted to talk to him, but couldn't think of a way to begin. I wasn't sure if he knew about my accident, and if not I decided that I didn't want him hearing it from someone else. I wanted to be the one to tell him.

But I was getting stuck on the words.

"Abby, what is it?"

He must have noticed my expression.

I inhaled. I hated talking about it.

"Did you know I was in an accident a few years ago?"

He was quiet for a minute, but his face did the talking.

"Yeah. They told us right after they decided to hire you. Something about you being in a car crash coming back from the mountain and it took you a long time to recover. I have to say though, I never would have known. I mean, you seem normal to me."

That stung a little, and he realized it right away.

"Sorry. That was stupid. What I meant was, the way they told us, I thought it was really serious. I was expecting you to have lots of scars, you know?"

"Yeah, that makes sense," I said. "And they didn't tell you anything else?"

"They also told us about your friend. The guy who died in the accident. I'm wondering if that's the guy you were talking about. You know, when I first asked you out to dinner."

My heart took off as I tried desperately to hold back the tears that were pooling in my eyes. I looked at Ty and nodded.

"Yeah," I said. "Jesse. We'd been best friends since fourth grade."

We sat quiet for a moment, both sinking in my deep pool of sadness. I stared out the window watching people walk by and trying to pull myself together.

"I'm so sorry, Abby," he said. "You can always talk about him to me. I'm your friend."

I nodded, but kept my eyes outside. I didn't want to talk to Ty about Jesse, but I was glad that he offered and that he knew who Jesse was now. And how much I missed him.

"Okay," I said. "I'll be right back. I promise I won't leave."

I stood up and tried to smile. When I turned the corner I ran to the bathroom, washed my face, and tried to calm down. In a few minutes, I was okay and walked back out. Ty was waiting up at the front and had already paid the bill.

"Hey, I thought I was taking *you* out to dinner, remember?"

"No way," he said. "This is my treat."

"Thanks," I said. "How about that hike?"

"Oh, yeah, I'd love to if you still want to go."

"Let's go."

I wasn't done talking. I decided to tell him everything else. That's what good friends did. They told each other their stories.

Chapter 23

"You want to walk up the trail or take the road?" I asked, handing him a water bottle from the back seat. I always kept a large supply of them for soccer. I took one too and we started walking toward the trail signs.

"Not the road," Ty said. "Unless there's some sort of advantage."

"Only in winter when there aren't any cars. Let's go up the trail."

We started climbing.

"I still can't believe you haven't been up to the top of Pilot Butte yet. You never even drove up?"

"No," Ty said. "I've been meaning to, just haven't had the chance. I did watch the firework show earlier this month."

"It's intense at the beginning, but it'll get better in a few minutes," I said.

Ty smiled. He didn't seem to be struggling at all.

It was only about a mile to the top. We kept climbing and rounding the butte and in about 20 minutes we were standing up at the observation platform. Three cars were parked and a few tourists were taking pictures. We read all the signs identifying the landmarks in the distance.

It was a perfect evening. The sky was still light and there were no clouds.

"Jeez, you can see so many mountains from up here. It must be the entire Cascade Range spread out before us."

"Yeah," I said. "It's a great view."

I pointed out some other things.

"This is amazing."

As we headed back down, I started telling him more about the accident. I told him about the lake I had drowned in, and about being dead before Dr. Mortimer brought me back to life. I told him how I couldn't see colors anymore and about how for more than a year I could only walk. And about how I barely finished my senior year in high school.

Ty listened and didn't say much of anything while I talked. We had made it almost all the way down by the time I finished.

"So you had one of those near death experiences?"

I checked on his energy waves. They were the same, white and shooting off around him. He wasn't upset or bothered about any of it. He wasn't making any judgments. I was relieved.

"Yeah," I said. "Kate was at the hospital, sitting with my body and waiting for the morgue guy to come and get me when I woke up."

"Oh, my God, that's some serious stuff right there."

I unlocked his door and walked around and got inside. As I started the car, Ty reached over and put his hand on mine.

"Thanks for telling me," he said. "I mean it. That is something crazy you went through. Honestly, I had no idea. I'm really, really sorry about throwing you in the water. Now it's making more sense. I feel like an idiot. I had no idea. They just said you were in a car accident."

"No worries," I said.

We drove back over to the rafting company, listening to the radio and not saying too much. When I pulled in next to his car and parked, he leaned over and gave me a hug.

110

"Thanks, Abby."

"Hey, I'm the one who needs to thank you for dinner."

"No, I mean thank you for telling me what happened," he said. "It means a lot that you shared all that with me."

I was glad that he knew now. It was a hard thing to talk about, especially with people I didn't know so well. But Ty was different. It felt like he was a real friend and that I could trust him. Completely.

Chapter 24

Kate was leaving for Portland early Monday morning and Dr. Mortimer was going to be dropping off his stuff sometime during the day. She had already given him a key and the alarm code and stocked the refrigerator with some sort of green juice he liked to drink before work.

"Bye, Abby," Kate whispered, sticking her head through my bedroom door.

It was still dark outside.

"Wait," I said.

I got up and walked over to my desk and handed her a sketch of the woman I had drawn the night before. It wasn't great, but at least it would give her an idea about what she looked like in a general sort of way.

"Thanks. This will help. Remember, I'll be sending over the pictures tonight, so look at them when you can and let me know. Also, if I were you, I wouldn't... well, how should I put this?"

"I know, got it," I said. "Don't talk about any of this ghost business with Dr. Mortimer."

"Yeah, it's probably for the best. At least for now, if you know what I mean. Otherwise, he'll ship you back to Dr. Krowe while I'm gone."

I smiled.

"And remember that I'm staying with Erin. You have her phone number, right?"

"Yeah, I have everything. Say hi for me."

"Okay. *Ciao* for now. I'll be back tomorrow night. Hopefully we'll learn some new things about your ghost."

I was too wired to get back to sleep, so I poured a cup of coffee and sat in the living room watching the morning light fill up the room. It was exciting to think that we might actually make some progress and find out about the ghost.

I thought about Ty as I got ready for work. He had texted me a couple times over the weekend just to say hi and tell me what he was doing. I had liked going out with him. It had been a good dinner and hike and I found myself thinking about him often. He really was a nice guy and I hoped that we could be friends. I hoped that it would be enough.

I got to work and saw him hanging out by the van.

"Hey, Abby," he said, smiling.

"Hey."

I helped him load up some gear as the other guides arrived. We got into the van and drove up to the river.

In my first group, a friendly family from Kansas with parents, three little kids, and a grandma were in my boat. I had a little trouble with the second group. Two teenagers were loud and obnoxious, but Ty helped me out with them, pulling them aside when we were scouting. I could hear him whispering that he would leave them there if they didn't shape up. The boys stared at the river while he talked. I could tell they really wanted to go down the rapids and promised to behave.

I was a little tired as we pushed off for the final run. There were three couples from different states in the raft. They were all pretty quiet and reserved, but I didn't mind. I could save my wildlife speech for the groups in the morning.

I noticed instantly that the water felt rougher and stronger than it had all day. Wild. Faster. Unsettled.

A strong current pulled us down the first set of rapids and I saw a new whirlpool forming on the right as we flew by. My stomach tensed and my heart raced.

"Be careful out there," Ty whispered after pulling off to scout Big Eddy. "It feels different. Try to follow where I go and remember what we talked about at dinner. Keep your eyes open and prepare for the unexpected."

"Got it."

I still felt confident. I would have to be careful, but I was determined to get through the rest of the run smoothly.

We got back into the rafts and Ty went first. I followed from a distance. As I back paddled, I saw something flash up ahead in the thin layer of mist right before the big drop.

It was her. Standing in the middle of the river, her eyes large and furious, staring at me.

"Oh, my God," I whispered, trying to catch my breath.

And then trying to breathe. The current was sweeping us forward. My stomach crashed as I stared at her. We were headed right toward her. She just stood there, in the middle of the river, full of fury, with those eyes. Those eyes.

I had to refocus and tried just to pay attention to getting in the right channel and shooting through Big Eddy. But I started thinking about our training and what they had told us about a raft from another company hitting a boulder at a bad angle in these rapids and flipping. One of the tourists had nearly drowned and a kid broke a leg.

But it was too late to turn back. I had to figure it out, had to go forward.

A huge wave suddenly pulled us to the left sharply, rocking us and banging the raft up against the big boulder before the first drop, close to where she was standing. I yelled at my group to paddle and steered us straight again.

"Harder," I shouted over the deafening sound of the water.

We had passed through her, but then she was up ahead again, standing on a large rock, overlooking the last drop. I whispered to her, pretty sure nobody on the boat could hear.

"We're working on it," I said. "Leave me alone."

But she just glared.

Suddenly the raft tilted and then turned around. We were backwards on the river. I pushed the paddle down into the water, trying to get us straight. But it was too late. I had to stop trying, because if we went down sideways now, the river would flip us.

My heart pounded in my chest. There was no choice but to go downriver backwards and blind and hope for the best.

"Paddles out," I yelled at the tourists.

I turned around in my seat, watching and paddling the best I could. Water crashed over the sides of the raft. I couldn't see anything, just large white waves flying up all around us. Then we dropped, listing badly to the right as we went full speed into the next wave.

"Damn it!" I said.

I knew it was out of my hands. The fast water took us down and there was nothing more to do but hope that we didn't land in the whirlpool or hit a large boulder.

But I wasn't as scared anymore. My breath was even now, and my nerves under control.

"We're not going into the water," I said to myself in a low voice. "Not today."

Another drop.

"Everyone lean to the left," I shouted. "Quick!"

We all leaned just in time. The final wave took us and spit us out into the calm section of the river, still facing backward.

Everybody cheered, including me, as I turned us around.

Ty had been watching us. He must have known I was having some trouble.

"Good job," he said.

I weakly returned his thumbs up. My mouth was bone dry and I sat there, unable to move for a minute. I thanked everyone for listening so well. I could tell they were happy to be done with the rapids. I couldn't blame them. I felt the same way.

But fear surged through me as I thought about her. She had seemed so angry and had distracted me right before the biggest set of rapids on the river.

Had she done that on purpose? Had she wanted me to flip into the river? Or worse?

I caught my breath, scooped some water in my hat and dumped it over my head. I thought about what Kate had said when she asked if the ghost was dangerous. When she asked if she had done anything to me.

I wasn't sure anymore.

I had never been so happy to see the take-out spot. I said goodbye to my group, trying to act casual. All of them had gray energy around them. It hadn't been fun, going backwards down the rapids. If they had been those teenage boys, it would have been a different story. But I was pretty sure that some of these people would complain back at the office.

We watched the bus take them away. I was exhausted and still shaking a little and eager to get home. I grabbed some paddles and loaded them.

Ty came up to me.

"Abby, you did good. Really good. It was pretty mean out there and bottom line, nobody took a bath."

I shrugged.

"The raft just turned around so quickly. I didn't have time to get it straight again."

"Just like I said, you have to be prepared for anything. And you did great. It might not have been the prettiest river run ever, but you got through it and nobody fell in and nobody got hurt. You did exactly right."

I started shaking hard and he rubbed my shoulders. Then he went into the bus and came back with a sweatshirt that had the University of Montana mascot on it.

"Here, put this on," he said. "You're freezing."

I put it on and, still shivering, walked over to a sunny spot and stood there for a few minutes. Then I helped them load up. I wanted to get home. I wanted to look through those pictures.

It was time to get her off my back.

Chapter 25

As I pulled up, I saw Dr. Mortimer's black BMW in the driveway.

I was still shaking from seeing her ghost and going backwards down the rapids. I didn't know what it meant, didn't know if she had really tried to hurt me. But whatever the reason for her being there, I felt a new urgency about finding her. I hoped she would be in the pictures that Kate was sending over.

As I collected my stuff, I thought of Jesse. More and more I questioned whether I had really seen him. He didn't look like a ghost. He didn't look like her. He wasn't terrifying.

She had been angrier than ever, her face burning with a desperation and intensity that I hadn't seen before. It had been a little while since I was up on the lava cliff. Maybe she thought that I had forgotten. Or I had changed my mind. Maybe she didn't know that I had been going through files and pictures, trying to find out who she was and learn her story.

I wasn't going to tell Dr. Mortimer about it, or even Kate for that matter.

I put a smile on my face and opened the front door.

"Dr. Mortimer," I said, trying to sound normal.

"Abby," he said.

He got up from the sofa.

I threw my bag down by the coat rack and walked into the living room with him. He had been watching the news. The weather guy with the giant shirt sleeves was saying that it would be hot the next few days, with plenty of blue skies.

Blue skies. It had been so long since I had seen a blue sky.

"So how was the river today?" he said.

His voice was a little off and I figured he must have picked up on something. I probably wasn't doing such a great job at hiding the fear I was feeling inside. I tried harder.

"It was a tough one, actually. Most days are great. But, you know, can't always please everybody. Some lady lost her hat and gave me a hard time."

We sat down and I slid off my sandals.

"I have that too, at the hospital all the time. It's a drag, sometimes, huh? Dealing with unhappy people."

"You lose people's hats too?" I said, working in a joke. He smiled.

"We lose all sorts of things. You don't want to know, trust me."

I just remembered that I had planned on cooking dinner for him, but I really didn't feel like it at all. I needed a nice cup of tea that could chase away the chills still crawling all over my insides, and then a good, long black and white movie.

"I'm going to change and then make you dinner. I hope you're hungry."

"Oh," Dr. Mortimer said.

He looked a little sad.

"I'm sorry. I was just trying to help out. I ordered a pizza. I figured you'd be tired and hungry when you got home. It'll be here in a few minutes."

"I can't even tell you how great that sounds," I said. "I'll be back."

I got up and walked toward my room.

"So, you're all set up in Kate's room and everything?" I asked, turning back around." Do you need anything?"

"I'm good. I have to leave in about an hour, though."

"Okay, I'll be fast."

I was already feeling better, and realized that maybe it was because Dr. Mortimer was here. It was nice having someone at home when I came back at the end of the day. Kate was hardly ever able to do that.

Although I was anxious to take a quick look at my email, I didn't. I headed back out to the kitchen. Dr. Mortimer had set the table with plates, poured sodas, and was dishing out the slices already.

"Do you ever get used to that crazy night shift schedule?" I asked.

"No, not at all actually. When I first started out I thought, no problem. I'll be used to this in a few weeks, maybe a month. But all these years later and I'm not even close to being used to it. I still have trouble falling asleep in the daylight and I have a heck of a time not yawning a blue streak after three in the morning."

"Kate says you want to be a pediatrician?"

"Oh, she remembered that?"

His eyes glazed over for a moment.

"Yeah, I still want to do that. I would have to go back to school, but I'd like to specialize in pediatrics sometime down the road."

I nodded and smiled, thinking he would make a great children's doctor.

I noticed Dr. Mortimer's energy suddenly turned gray. He was nervous. I had a feeling he wanted to talk about something and I hoped it wasn't any bad news about Nathaniel. I couldn't take that on right now. Not with what I already had on my plate.

"Hey," he said, trying to sound casual. "I have a question for you. But you can tell me if I'm out of line. I promise it won't hurt my feelings."

I was relieved. I knew it was about Kate.

"Sure. What is it?"

"I'm kind of at a loss with Kate lately and need some advice."

I didn't want to say too much or make her mad. She wouldn't like me talking about her with Dr. Mortimer. But I also wanted to help them.

"Sure," I said, hesitating a little.

"Well." He paused, fighting to find the right words. "I'm just wondering. Do you think if I can find Nathaniel and bring him in that I'll have a chance with her again? I'm just not sure. She has that boyfriend and I'm trying to get a reading on that but can't really. What do you think?"

I thought about it for a minute. He turned and looked at me, waiting for an answer. His eyes were so serious and I could see that he was really deeply in love with Kate. Still. After all this time.

But I didn't know what to say. And I didn't really know the answer. She could be stubborn sometimes.

"I'm not really sure," I finally said. "I know she…" I stopped and came up with some new words. "I know she really cares about you, Dr. Mortimer. And that she isn't so in love with Colin. But, you're right. I don't know exactly what it would take for her to let all that stuff go."

I did have a strong feeling about what it would take, but I wasn't going to say it. I was thinking that a bullet through his brother's head would satisfy Kate. And maybe nothing else.

Whatever I had just said seemed to lift his spirits a little.

121

"Thanks. That helps. I know there's not an easy answer. Anyway, I better focus on getting Nathaniel first, right? Then, hopefully, all this relationship stuff will just fall into place."

"Yeah," I said. "I think that would be a big part of her coming back around. Getting Nathaniel."

"Well, okay then. I better get ready."

He walked out of the kitchen and I heard Kate's bathroom door close.

I took my soda over to the sofa and sat down, flipping the channels.

"Okay, Abby," Dr. Mortimer said, walking toward the door.

I was expecting scrubs, but he was more dressed up than usual.

"You can reach me at the ER anytime. You have all the numbers. And I'll be back in the morning just after seven or so. Sorry I couldn't get any time off. I tried, but they've cut the staff tremendously this summer and it was too short notice. I hope it helps somewhat, me staying here during the day."

"It does," I said. "It was great seeing you tonight. Plus it makes Kate happy."

I walked him to the door and said goodbye.

After watching his car drive away, I brought out my laptop and checked my phone. Kate had left a message, telling me she had downloaded the pictures and I should have them in an email. There were a lot of pictures to go through.

As I scanned the photos, that same heaviness crept back that I had felt before when I looked at those other missing women. It went fast. Most of the women didn't match up to her at all. They either had the wrong hair color or face shape. There were a lot of them. Too many.

I muted the TV and turned on some music. Gladys Knight and the Pips started singing about being someone's woman.

And then, two women later, I found her.

It was the eyes that I noticed first. Even when she was alive, she had those stark, serious eyes. They stared right through me even from an old photograph.

Her name was Annabelle Harrison. She was 27 years old and had lived in Portland, Oregon. She had gone missing on November 9, 2003. And she was last seen at a grocery store.

I couldn't believe it. I sat, staring at her picture and reading all her information over and over again.

She had the same long, dark hair, but it was styled nicely in the picture, and flipped up at the ends. The picture looked like she was at a party of some sort, with a large banner in the background. And even though she was smiling, she had the same haunted look that most of the missing women had in their photos: a hollowness in their eyes, a vacant expression on their faces. An eternal sadness in their souls, almost like anticipation of what was to come. Like they knew.

My stomach tightened as I phoned Kate. A small part of me was happy to have found her, but mostly I just felt a terrible sadness. *Annabelle*. It was odd that she had a name now, odd to see her filled out. Living.

I ran my finger over her picture, thinking about her name. Annabelle. It was a beautiful name. I thought about her parents when they named her and all the hopes and dreams they must have had for her, never dreaming she would end up at the bottom of a river 27 short years later.

I sighed, waiting for Kate to pick up. In a way finding her made all this insanity real. It wasn't just my imagination.

It was official. I really did see ghosts.

Chapter 26

"Really? You found her? That's incredible! Awesome. Wait, hold on one second."

I could hear Kate talking to someone in the background. "Okay, sorry, I'm at Pioneer Place shopping with Erin. She's in the dressing room. But I found a place to sit and go over the photos. I have my iPad here. Which one is she?"

I told her. She pulled up the information a minute later.

"Oh, my God," she said before going quiet for a moment. "Wow, she looks just like the sketch you gave me. It's eerie."

"Yeah, for me too," I said. "You know, I thought I would feel better, but I don't. I just feel really sad. What do you think happened to her?"

"That's what I'm going to find out tomorrow. But, Abby, you should focus on the good in all this. Remember that you're going to be helping out her loved ones. It's still an unsolved case, and I know how especially heartbreaking those are for the families. It's a terrible thing not knowing what happened to someone you love. You're giving them so much."

When Kate said that, I thought about Jesse. That was exactly it. He was like one of those that went missing. And it was a terrible feeling. I didn't know what had happened to him. He had just vanished that day, and I wasn't sure if he was ever coming back.

"You're right."

"Hey, did Ben make it over there today?"

"Oh, yes. We had a pizza. It was nice seeing him."

"Good. I'm glad he's there, but it's too bad you have to be home alone tonight. Is there a friend or somebody you could go hang out with for a while?"

"Yeah, maybe," I said.

I was thinking of Claire. At least I could write to her. Maybe that would help shake some of this awful feeling.

"Good. Do it, Abby. This is great news. I have my work cut out for me tomorrow. I'll try to find out what I can before heading home. I'm going to contact her family. Maybe they can help me get those divers out to the river."

"Sounds good," I said.

"It's all good. Keep your eyes on the prize."

"I will," I said. "Bye, Kate. Say hi to Erin and thanks again for everything."

"I'll call you later tonight. Bye."

Eyes on the prize. I wasn't sure what that meant. Annabelle was dead. I couldn't see any prizes coming out of that. The time for prizes had passed.

I tossed down the phone and it bounced off the sofa, landing on the ground with a thud.

It had been a day from hell. At least, that's how I was feeling. Bad. Feeling like I used to feel. Like I didn't belong in my life.

Like I was a freak.

Chapter 27

I needed some fresh air to change my mood. It was only seven and I thought I would go over to the park and watch a soccer game. I knew Jack and Tim played on a different team Monday nights. I put on my shoes and brought my cleats and shin guards, just in case they needed an extra player.

As I was driving over, I realized that part of my sadness had to do with Jesse. If I was able to see ghosts, then why couldn't I see him anymore? Where was he? I couldn't stop thinking about what Claire had written, the part about how Jesse might have moved on.

I knew it was selfish but I wanted him and needed him. With every passing day, I loved him more. But now I wondered if I didn't love a ghost, but rather something else. A figment of my imagination.

I saw Jack's large pickup truck near the edge of the grass where it was always parked. It almost seemed like he lived here. I always saw his truck in the exact same place. He was seriously obsessed with the game.

I walked up to the grass. They were in the second half. Jack saw me on the sidelines after a few minutes and waved.

"Hey, AC, what are you doing here?" he asked, chasing down the ball as it bounced out of bounds. He threw it in to a teammate and ran back on the field.

"Thought I'd just watch a game for a change," I said.

"Good! We'll talk after. Don't disappear."

It felt good to have friends. It was a new experience this year and I liked it. It wasn't even like I was going to tell Jack anything, but I already felt better being outside and saying hello.

The ref blew the whistle and the game ended. Everybody headed over to the sidelines. Jack had his usual entourage of friends following. Some of them were talking under their breaths, mad at the other team.

"You okay, AC?" he asked.

"Just needed some air. Had a little time to kill. Kate's out of town and I didn't feel like being by myself."

Jack wiped off his face with his sleeve.

"Wanna come out with us? I'm supposed to meet up with Bree for a beer. Why don't you come along?"

That was the one thing that was a little strange this year about my new friends. They were all older than me and usually went out for drinks.

"Oh, I'm good. I think I'll just head home now. I enjoyed watching the game. You guys won, right? Why were those guys angry?"

Jack looked to the side where his teammates were collecting their stuff and leaving. The other two teams about to play were already on the field. The sidelines were crowded, full of soccer players.

"There were some real hacks out there tonight. The ref let them get away with a lot of crap. Hey, did you see my new jersey?"

Jack pulled it down and turned around, smiling. He knew I'd hate it. It was a Sergio Ramos Real Madrid shirt.

"Like I would say something about him," I said. "Something nice, I mean. Come on. I can't think of a dirtier player, except maybe van Bommel. Come to think of it, he would fit right in out here."

"Sergio's just tenacious, that's all," he said. "You'll come around, AC."

He laughed as I shook my head. He was just trying to make me mad.

"But seriously. You don't look like yourself or something. You okay?"

"Just a hard day," I said. "But I feel better."

We talked for a few more minutes. I was tired now, really tired. I headed home and locked everything up and got ready for bed.

But first I had to write Claire and give her an update about how Kate had found Annabelle, and also about me seeing her so angry on the river. As I started writing, I stopped. Claire had written me in the morning, but I had missed it. Goose bumps crept up my arms as I read her email.

"You're in danger, Abby. Danger! I'm picking up on something. Not sure what. But for God's sake, be careful."

I cringed. Claire had known. She knew that Annabelle's ghost was angry and was coming after me on the river. I should have checked her message before leaving in the morning.

I wrote back, telling her everything and asking for help. I wanted Claire to tell her that we were close to wrapping up the case. I wanted her to tell Annabelle to leave me alone.

I headed to bed, dreading the river in the morning.

Chapter 28

I swallowed my fear as I grabbed my paddle.

Focus, I told myself.

Going backwards down the rapids had left me freaked out. Seriously freaked out. It brought back so much, too much. As I paddled us out into the calm waters, all I could think about was the dark place where I couldn't breathe anymore. The darkness at the bottom of that lake.

It left me wondering if I really was crazy for being out here all day, for taking this job as a river guide. Even though most days I felt good, maybe I hadn't thought it through. Maybe I was just trying to prove something. Like some tragic hero. Like William Holden getting killed at the end of all those old movies.

All it would take was one small mistake in the whitewater, one mistake to send me back to those waters. Kate was right. I had no business being out here. What was I thinking?

And there was no one to talk to about it. I was totally alone. I couldn't tell Ty or Dr. Mortimer or Jack about the ghost on the river and I couldn't tell Kate that Annabelle had tried to hurt me. And although I wanted to think that she hadn't done it intentionally, I really had no idea. I couldn't be sure one way or the other.

I just prayed that I wouldn't see her again.

My first group was a large family from Chicago. We got in and after I gave them instructions, it was a relief to feel that the flow of the water was back at its usual pace. I still wasn't sure what had happened yesterday. That part wasn't Annabelle's fault. After all, she couldn't control how much water was released from the dam upstream.

I led us through Big Eddy, facing forward this time and full of a new fear I couldn't quite shake. But I did well, catching the right channel and shooting the rapids with just the right amount of thrills. When we were out in the calmer section, Ty gave me one of his famous thumbs up.

"Nice," he shouted, his voice echoing off the rocks and down the river.

The rest of the day was like that. Easy, really. And normal. Like it had been all summer. Done right with no problems. As we loaded up to go home, Ty walked up.

"Hey. You know, we didn't really get a chance to talk. I just wanted to say what a great time I had going on that hike."

"Me too," I said.

"Maybe we can do it again. Somewhere different. Like up in the mountains. I've been on some great hikes up there. How about Green Lakes?"

"Yeah," I said. "I'd love to. Green Lakes is killer."

After work, I headed over to the park. I wandered around, checking out the courts and the running path through the woods. Helping Annabelle wasn't helping. She wasn't getting me any closer to finding Jesse. She wasn't stringing me along for the money because she wasn't charging. I knew she was doing her best. Maybe there just wasn't anything anyone could do. Maybe it was all hopeless.

I couldn't shake the feeling. Why had Jesse vanished?

I thought for a moment he might be mad about Ty. But that didn't explain why he hadn't been around all that time before. I walked the path through the forest and when I was by myself, I spoke to him.

"I love you, Jesse," I said, softly. "Please come back."

I hoped my words would cross between our worlds and reach him.

"I still need you. Please come back to me."

Only a gentle breeze answered. I continued on the path looking for him, trying to fight the strong feeling, stronger now than the waves at Big Eddy, that I would never again see him.

Chapter 29

I didn't see Dr. Mortimer when I got home. He had already left for work. I texted him, apologizing again about not being able to cook dinner while he was staying over. I saw that he had left all his stuff, probably in case Kate had to stay in Portland another day. He wrote back a little later.

"How about a rain check? I can email you my schedule."

I sent back a smiley face.

I headed over to my soccer game, grateful that I was playing. I needed to get my mind off things, get lost in the grass, and only think about a soccer ball at my feet. My brain was on overdrive and I needed a break. I needed a goal.

I scored twice and we beat the Pirates 3-1.

"So close to a hat trick, AC," Jack said. "Nice game."

"You too, Jack. You had some great moves out there tonight."

He smiled as he shoved his ball into his soccer bag.

"You seem back to your old self," he said as he looked at me.

I didn't like it when people stared at me that way, but I knew he didn't mean anything by it.

"Yeah. Better day on the river."

"Good," he said.

I picked up my bag and checked the time. Kate would be home soon and I could hardly wait.

Chapter 30

Kate called before reaching the mountain pass and said she wouldn't be home until after midnight.

"Sorry, Abby. I got a late start. I was talking with Erin. But just go to bed. We can talk in the morning."

I could hear Diana Krall playing her piano in the background. It made me a little nervous, her driving back at these hours. I knew she must be tired.

"Did you get some coffee?"

"Got it right here. Hey, don't worry. It's a beautiful night and I'm pumped up. And there are still plenty of cars on the road."

"Good."

"Okay, I'm about to lose reception. If you're sleeping when I get home, I'm not going to wake you. I want you to be rested in the morning."

"I'll be up," I said. "I want to hear everything."

After we hung up, I got my blanket and pillow and put them on the sofa. I wasn't going to take any chances. If I stayed in the living room the front door would wake me. I found an old film noir on Turner Classics called *The Killers*. Annabelle looked a little like a young Ava Gardner, I thought before slipping into a deep sleep.

It felt like only a minute had gone by when the front door woke me. I met Kate as she came in with her bags.

"You did it. You stayed up."

"Of course," I said, yawning and then smiling. I went into the kitchen and made tea while she changed. It was already after one in the morning. The kettle boiled and I poured hot water into two mugs, sliding in decaf Earl Gray teabags, and put them on the table along with some cookies. In a few minutes Kate wandered in, her hair up in a ponytail.

"Wow, it's good to be home," she said. "It's a long drive back sometimes. That stretch from Warm Springs to Bend goes on forever."

She sat down and blew on her tea, cupping it in her hands.

"Boy, we're very lucky people. Sometimes you forget."

"That's true," I said. "We are lucky."

Kate seemed a little shaken, but it wasn't a surprise. She took her investigations seriously and they always affected her.

"Hey, before we start, how has work been?" she asked.

"Good," I said, shoving a cookie in my mouth.

She was preoccupied so she didn't pick up on the lie. I wasn't going to tell her about Annabelle scaring me on the river or about how I had gone down backwards on the Big Eddy.

"And how's Ty?" she asked, smiling.

Kate had been ridiculously happy when I told her I went out to dinner with him.

"We're just friends."

She nodded. And smiled some more.

"I just texted Ben to let him know that I made it back okay. He'll probably drop by in the morning to pick everything up."

135

Kate took a cookie and walked out of the kitchen. She returned with her computer and a large file stuffed full of papers.

"Oh, Erin says hi," she said as she pulled out the papers and put them on the kitchen table. "She also says she misses you. She wants you to come visit her in Portland. She says being in a big city would be good for you."

After my accident, when I was having all those problems with strangers, I sometimes talked to Erin about how much I hated living in Bend, about how it felt like the walls were closing in around me. She always told me that the world was a big place and not to settle for small things. And if I was unhappy, all I had to do was pick up and go somewhere else, try something different.

Things were much better now, although I hadn't had a chance to tell her because she moved last year. We emailed back and forth once in a while, but it wasn't often. I always really liked that advice she gave me and kept it close to my heart.

"Okay, ready?" Kate said.

"Let's do it," I said.

She handed me a large photograph.

"Here's a picture of Annabelle Harrison and her husband and son, four months before she disappeared."

There was no mistake. It was her. Annabelle was the ghost who was haunting me.

I stared for a few moments at the photo. It was one of those family portraits taken by a fancy studio, the kind that stamped their signature at the bottom of all the pictures. Annabelle and a light-haired kid were sitting together, her arm draped over his shoulder. A man in a suit stood stiffly behind them. Although they were all smiling, none of them seemed that happy.

"Jacob is seven there. He's fifteen now. And that's her husband, Derek."

I ran my fingers over the picture.

"It was taken in August and she went missing in November."

I nodded and then put the picture aside.

"And here's her driver's license. This was in *The Oregonian* files. I was able to get photocopies of anything I wanted. Erin helped out with that."

I held the paper in my hands. My sketch really had been good, looking close to the picture on her license. She had that same, serious expression, that same long dark hair. I read over her stats. She was 5'6 and 135 pounds with green eyes.

"I wasn't able to interview her husband. He's an attorney and was in court all day. But we did talk on the phone and said I could email him with any questions. He seems interested in what I'm doing, although he didn't have any idea why there would be a Bend connection in her disappearance. He said they had never been to Central Oregon before."

"So he's a nice guy?" I asked.

I wasn't picking up on that at all. In fact, as I looked at him and touched him with my fingers, I was picking up on the opposite.

"I wouldn't say that. He's abrupt and cocky but he's an attorney, so what can you expect."

Kate stood up and pulled out her notes.

"And there's something else about him."

I looked up.

"He was a suspect," she said. "No, wait. I mean a person of interest, to be exact. He was never charged and he hired a bigwig firm immediately. But at the time the police were interested in him. I talked with the detectives who had worked the case all those years ago and they said they searched the home several times, but never found anything.

And of course, there was no body. Annabelle just vanished into the Portland night and the case went cold."

"They found nothing?" I asked. "If he did murder her, he must be good."

I thought of all the TV shows Kate loved watching and about how the suspects always left some evidence no matter how hard they tried to clean up after themselves. Between DNA and fingerprints and blood splatters, it seemed almost impossible to get away with murder these days.

"He specializes in criminal law defense, so he would have an inside track on what to do," Kate said.

She looked up from her notes.

"The detectives each had a different feeling about him. One thought he did it, that he killed his wife and was able to get rid of her body successfully. But the other one thought he was innocent. This was his quote: 'He's an asshole, but an innocent asshole.'"

I nodded as I looked at her son again. Kate sat back down in the chair and finished her tea.

"You sure didn't pick a simple ghost, Abby. It's a complicated case, to say the least."

"Yeah, that was my feeling," I said. "She just seems so angry."

"What do you mean so angry?"

"It's in her eyes. And in her energy. Mad. Brooding. Impatient. She seems to really want my help, but there's this crazy intensity to her, too. Like something has happened. I can't figure it out."

Kate put her mug down on the table and looked at me.

"She hasn't done anything to you, has she?"

"No, nothing like that." I noticed my voice went up a little and hoped she hadn't picked up on it. "But it'll be good to help her and move on. I think the most important thing she wants is to be found."

"That makes sense," Kate said. "Her son doesn't know what happened to her."

She handed me another paper.

"This is the missing person's report, filed by the husband. He said that she never returned from the supermarket. He called the police at midnight and then came in and filed the paperwork after the required waiting period."

I quickly read over it.

"They thought it was a stranger abduction at first, like maybe a kidnapping-for-ransom scenario. She was driving a nice car and they were prominent in the community."

"Ransom? Really?"

"It's not like they were super wealthy, but they were doing pretty well. They were well known in political circles. Both were active in the Democratic Party in Portland. Mr. Harrison was up-and-coming and being groomed for office. And Annabelle volunteered at all the local campaigns, rallies, and fundraisers.

"Interesting," I said.

"So anyway her Audi was found in the store's parking lot. Nobody remembers seeing her in the market and there's no record of a purchase."

"You said *at first* they thought that it was an abduction. They don't think it was anymore?"

"No," Kate said. "Not after finding out that she was having an affair."

"What?"

My heart sank.

"Rumors were that she was having an affair, possibly with one of the other campaign volunteers."

"Really?" I said. "Wow."

"Harrison finding out about it would give him a good motive," Kate said. "It would be embarrassing and might even ruin his career."

I sat quiet for a few minutes, reading over all the papers and thinking.

"Is it kind of a letdown?" Kate finally asked, breaking the silence. "Her having the affair?"

"A little I guess," I said. "But it doesn't matter what she did. She didn't deserve to be killed. It's all so sad, that's all."

"Yeah," Kate said. "Of course, Mr. Harrison has his own theory. After the news broke about her affair, he told police that Annabelle left the country with her mysterious boyfriend and they are living it up in Mexico or the Caribbean. And that's also what he's told his son."

"The bastard," I said. Now Annabelle's anger was making sense. "I don't think she would just leave her son like that."

"He told the detectives that she never even wanted to be a mother," Kate said. She pulled some more pictures out and handed them to me. "The detectives let me copy these. What do you think?"

I looked through the stack of photos. They were of Annabelle and Jacob. In one shot, she was on the merry-go-round with him when he was a toddler. In another they were building a sand castle on the beach. Another one looked like it was his first day of school. That intensity was gone from her face and her smile was real.

"I think she loved her son," I said. "That was wrong to tell him that."

"Yeah, seems like that would mess a kid up for life."

Kate stacked the papers back into a neat pile.

"But first things first," she said. "We've got to figure out a way of getting her off the bottom of the Deschutes River. The sheriff's not going to send in a diver just because you've seen a ghost. And I didn't find anyone in Portland who could ask them to look for her in the river. I need to think on this. We have to find a way, but not so to attract too much attention about knowing that she's down there."

I hadn't even thought about that. For some reason I was thinking that they would automatically send in the divers once Kate found out who the ghost was. Clearly I had been watching too many movies.

Kate yawned and stood up, stretching.

"But no more thinking tonight. Time for bed."

She said goodnight. I went through the motions of putting on my PJs and lying between the soft sheets, but there was no way I could fall asleep. I couldn't turn off my mind. It took hours before I finally drifted off, all the time thinking about Annabelle Harrison and wondering what had really happened to her.

Chapter 31

I was surprised that I wasn't tired the next morning. I must have been too excited.

Dr. Mortimer stopped by to get his stuff, but Kate was in the shower at the time. He seemed disappointed, but didn't want to wait.

"She's not usually that long," I said.

"Ah, no," he said, walking toward the door. "I better just get going. Say hi for me."

I walked with him out to his car.

"How about coming back for a party I'm throwing?"

"Sure. I'd love to. It's hard with my schedule, though. Let me know when it is and I'll try to make it."

"It'll be sometime next month. I'm flexible. If you can email me your schedule, I'll make sure to have it on your day off. I want you to meet my other friends. It would mean a lot to me."

He smiled.

"Sounds great," he said, opening the car door.

I waved as he drove away, pleased with my plan. It would be hard cooking for so many people, but I was already looking forward to it. I figured I'd invite the river guides and the soccer team.

I went back inside and got ready for work.

Kate was tagging along because she wanted to see where I thought Annabelle's body was located in the river. She drove behind me on the Cascades Highway, the road leading up the mountains. We passed The Seventh Mountain Resort and turned onto the bumpy dirt road that led down to our take-out spot on the river.

It was still pretty early and the parking lot was empty. It was nice seeing the river so quiet. Rare, really. It was peaceful when there weren't hundreds of tourists around. We walked over to the edge of the water.

"There," I said. "That's where I first saw her, floating right above the water."

"Man, that must have given you the creeps," Kate said.

"Yeah, it did."

I paused and then went on.

"And the second time I saw her she was up there, on that cliff across the river. But she was pointing to the same spot. It's got to be where she is."

Kate pulled her small camera out of her pocket and took some pictures from different angles. Then she stood for a while, staring.

"It's terrible, what happened to her," she said. "You know, I talked to one of her friends in Portland and she is so happy that I'm looking into Annabelle's disappearance. She said there was no way Annabelle would ever leave her son."

"Did you ask her about the affair?"

"Yeah," Kate said. "She didn't know anything about it. But you know, in my book, this mysterious lover should be as much a suspect as the husband."

"That's true," I said.

"By the way," she said. "I think I came up with an idea about how to get the divers out here."

143

"That was fast. How?"

"We have a photographer over at the newspaper from Hawaii who might be able to help. He's a scuba diver and goes up to some of the lakes on the weekends. I'm wondering if I can talk him in to going into the river and seeing what's down there. Maybe taking some pictures. If she's there, he can show what he has to the police. It could get the ball rolling."

"Do you think he'd do it?" I asked.

"Yeah, I do. Daniel's different from the usual photographers I have to deal with. He's got a lot of ambition. I'm going to ask him today."

"Sounds like a great idea. Let me know what he says."

I looked back over to the spot.

"Okay. Better get going. Man, this will be a pretty big story if they find her."

We walked back up to the cars. We were still the only ones in the dusty lot.

"Thanks again. For everything."

"Don't be silly," she said, looking around one more time.

There was a chill to the morning, but it was beautiful. The birds were singing and the sun was just making its way up. The light was beginning to dissolve the thin mist that hung over the dark water.

"It's sure nice out here," Kate said. "It makes sense why you want to be out here every day."

She got in her Subaru and rolled down the window.

"Bye," I said. "See you tonight."

"Stay safe out there."

I got in the Jeep and followed her out to the highway.

As I drove, I thought of Claire. It was odd, seeing ghosts like we did. There was so much I didn't understand. Like, how I was able to see them, but not really able to talk to

144

them. It seemed that she talked with spirits all the time. I wondered why it was so different for me.

And I wondered why I didn't have any problems talking to Jesse. At least when he had been around. So long ago now.

Chapter 32

I drove back to the Raft Adventures office, parked, and waited for the guides to show up before going inside. When everyone arrived, we signed in and drove up to the river.

I sat next to Ty on the way and listened as he talked about Montana and grizzly bears and about the close call he once had with a mother and her cubs.

"Hey, by the way, when are we doing another dinner?"

"I'm kind of busy this next week. I'm helping my sister with something," I said, knowing I needed to focus on Annabelle. "But how about after that?"

"All right, I guess," Ty said. "But I won't forget and I'm holding you to it."

My confidence on the water came back as I paddled and guided my groups through the whitewater all day. And that feeling of peace was back, too. I didn't see her ghost on any of the runs, and I had the feeling that she was being patient. At least, that's what I hoped.

I was doing the best I could to find her and I felt we were close. Annabelle had to understand that. Or not. That was beyond my control.

When I got home, I was surprised to find Kate out in the backyard. I wandered out after grabbing a soda. She was in the corner, by the trees, in the small little section of dirt. It had been completely overgrown all summer, but now the soil looked new and dark. She was surrounded by empty bags and lots of flowers in little plastic containers.

"Hey, Kate."

She took her ear buds out.

"Oh, hi, Abby."

She stood up and backed away, looking at her work.

"What do you think?"

"Nice," I said. "Kind of late in the season, though, isn't it?"

Kate looked at me.

"Yeah, I guess so. But I was driving home, and thought about how we always planted flowers out here when we were kids."

I remembered that it was usually Mom who did all the planting, and Kate and I messed around with the hose.

"Yeah, we did always have a nice flower garden back here. I haven't thought about it in a long time," I said.

"It is kind of late but they'll last for a little while. At least through September."

The flowers themselves looked nice. She had chosen a lot of different kinds, but of course I couldn't see any of the colors.

"Sorry you can't see them like they are," she said, pointing. "This one is purple, this one blue. And those over there are yellow."

I barely remembered what any of those colors looked like, but I tried to sound interested.

"You know, I couldn't stop thinking about Annabelle all day," Kate said. "It really made me sad. She was so young. And then the part about nobody knowing what happened to her and thinking she just ran off. It really got to me. It's just so awful."

She picked up a rake and started going over the dirt, evening it out. The trees swayed in the wind, casting omi-

147

nous shadows over the yard. Kate sat on her knees and started flipping the flowers out of the pots.

"Oh, by the way, Daniel was out on a shoot all day in Madras. But I left a message for him."

"Good," I said.

She wiped off her hands on her shirt.

"So I hear Ben is coming to your party."

Damn. I had wanted to tell her about it, but Dr. Mortimer had already spilled his guts. He must have been excited and wanted Kate to be there too. I tried to get a read on her emotions.

"Yeah," I said. "I was supposed to make him dinner when he was here, but ran out of time. I just wanted to make it up to him. It's not for a while. Hope that's okay."

She was quiet for a minute.

"Of course. It's nice, actually," she said, digging a hole.

"Hey, when are we going back out to the range?" I asked.

"Let's go soon. Good thinking. As busy as we are, we need to make time for it. It's important."

"Good. Okay, then," I said, heading inside.

"See you in a bit," she said, putting her music back in her ears.

Chapter 33

Kate called in the morning, catching me as I pulled into work.

"Abby, Daniel is in. He's excited about it, actually. I didn't even have to try and talk him into it. He says he has some new underwater photographic equipment he just got and wants to try it out. He's going down there tonight, before the sun goes down. All the rafters will be off the river by then."

It was great news. I was getting worried because if he wasn't going to do it, we didn't seem to have a Plan B.

"Can we come and watch?" I asked.

I had a soccer game, but I would skip it.

"Probably not," Kate said. "It would be better if we weren't around. If the police ever ask him what he was doing out there, he's going to tell them he was just trying out his new camera gear. But if we're there and they hear about it, it will complicate things."

That made sense.

"Okay," I said.

I couldn't wait to hear the news. I figured when I saw Kate after soccer, she'd probably know if Daniel had found anything in the river.

That night, our undefeated record went up in flames as we lost to the Blue Angels 4-1.

"Damn it," Jack said on the sidelines after the game. "All right, what say we start a new winning streak next game? On the plus side, we still have the best record in the league."

He was doing his best to put a spin on it, but I could tell he was taking it hard.

When I walked inside the house later, Kate was at the table, smiling.

"He got something, Abby," she said. "You were right. There's a body down there. Right where you rafters take out."

I took a breath. It was all real.

Chapter 34

When Kate got home Friday, she showed me copies of the pictures Daniel had taken and given to the police that morning.

I was nervous about looking at them, but she assured me it was okay.

"She's wrapped up," Kate said. "Like in plastic or something. But look, it's the same shape and size of a body."

I looked through the photos.

"Daniel says it's lodged in pretty good down there between some rocks, but he's confident that they'll be able to get her out. At least she's not under the rapids."

I nodded.

We headed out on our way back to the shooting range for some more practice. As we drove through the desert, we didn't say much.

There was a wait this time to get a spot, but it was worth it. Our aim was improving and that made Kate happy. She nailed the target, all her shots hitting either the chest or head. I had one good shot.

"Nice," she said, pulling the target off the clip.

It had gone through the head.

"That's what we're talking about!"

When we got home I wrote Claire, telling her everything, and asking about Jesse. I told her I really just wanted to know, and told her to tell me the truth. I was starting to doubt that I had really seen him for all those months after my accident. I asked her if she thought I had made him up.

She answered back late Sunday night.

Abby,
That's great news about Annabelle. You are very close.
I know with me, it took a while before I got better at seeing and hearing the spirits. I think it will be that way with you, too. You will hear the ghosts soon.
And don't give up on Jesse. I sense that he's close by. Of course, I could be wrong.
Claire

I was planning to be done with ghosts after we helped Annabelle, and her family knew the truth. But Claire's message made me think that I was just beginning with all this.

I hoped what she was saying about Jesse was true. But I doubted it more and more as time passed. I wondered if Jesse had even been a ghost at all.

Chapter 35

"That's great," Kate said, talking on the phone and pacing back and forth in front of the TV, blocking my view.

She was on the phone with the photographer.

"Thanks for calling, Daniel. And thanks again for all your help. I owe you big time."

I put down my bowl of cereal on the coffee table.

"The sheriff's department is sending out the divers tomorrow morning. They looked at the video footage and the photos and agreed that something is down there."

"That's awesome," I said.

I got up and gave her a high five.

"Daniel said that they're very interested. Of course, they think it's one of those other people missing here in Bend the last few years. But it doesn't matter. As long as they get her out of the river, our job is done."

"That was sure great that your friend helped out like that," I said.

Kate agreed.

"They'll close the river for the search," she said. "At least for the morning."

She grabbed her phone and called someone as she picked up her purse and headed out the door. I said goodbye, but I didn't know if she heard me.

I finished getting ready and went to work. When I got to the office, Amber and Ty were there.

"Hi," she said. "We were talking about the news we just heard. They're closing off the river tomorrow."

"Really?" I said, pretending to be surprised.

"Yeah," Ty said.

"I'm hoping it won't be for the entire day," she said. "I really need the money."

"I hear that," he said.

"Did they say why?" I asked.

"Nope," Amber said. "It's got to be something big, though."

"It's gotta be a body search," Ty said. "They did that once in Montana. Found a guy in the Flathead who had fallen in two years before, and 25 miles upriver. He was lodged in among some submerged trees, but they were able to finally pull him out. What was left of him anyway."

"Eew," Amber said. "Good story, Ty."

We got our gear and headed out to the van.

The currents were swift and stronger on the first few runs, reminding me of the last time I saw Annabelle on the river. But I was ready this time and did a good job steering us through the whitewater. We stayed facing forward.

When we got back to the office at the end of the day, the manager reminded us that there would be no work in the morning. They would be calling us with an update sometime before noon.

Chapter 36

When I got home, I was surprised to see Dr. Mortimer's car out front parked next to Kate's. It made me happy, until I realized that something must have happened.

I opened the door cautiously.

"Hey," I said.

They were both sitting at the dining room table. He stood up and smiled.

"Abby," he said. "We've been waiting for you. Good news."

I looked over at Kate. She was smiling too. I felt strange, like I had interrupted something.

"Hey," she said.

"Something about Annabelle?" I asked.

"Annabelle?" Dr. Mortimer said.

"Go ahead and tell her, Ben," she said.

He looked at me, his eyes dancing with excitement.

"It's Nathaniel. We got him. We know exactly where he is."

"Oh, my God, really?" I said, smiling ear to ear. "That's incredible."

"Let's sit down," Kate said.

We sat at the table and Dr. Mortimer told me the agency had found Nathaniel working in a Kenyan refugee camp.

"Look, I even have some pictures they faxed over. These were taken just a few days ago."

"I've seen it already, Abby. It's him, if you don't want to look."

"No, I want to," I said.

Dr. Mortimer handed me the photos.

"I was so excited. I rushed here right away. I wanted you two to know."

I took a deep breath and tried to calm down. I looked through the photos and then at Kate.

"Wow," I said, taking another breath. "It really is him."

It was hard to believe, but there he was. Nathaniel Mortimer looked the same as the last time I'd seen him when we confronted him about the murders in Bend. His long, black hair was still carefully slicked back in a neat ponytail. In the first two pictures he wore a doctor's coat and was treating patients. In the last one, he was standing in front of a tent, staring out.

That was the one that shot chills down the back of my neck. That look. It was the same exact look he had when we spoke in Dr. Mortimer's house. In the picture, he looked like a killer. Arrogant and aloof.

"I still don't understand what he's doing there," Kate said. "It just isn't like him."

"I don't either," Dr. Mortimer said. "But I'll find out."

I didn't really care. It felt good to know with certainty that he was far away. I hoped that it brought a little peace of mind to Kate too.

"So now what?" I asked.

"Now we work on building a case," he said. "The agency investigators already have all the files of the four murders here in Bend. They're going over everything."

He sat back in the chair, waiting for a reaction from Kate.

"I never did think the police department here tried very hard," she said. "I think those files must have something in them. Something that they overlooked."

"I know it's just the beginning, but I'm seeing this through to the end. Until Nathaniel has been brought to justice."

"That's great news," I said, handing back the papers.

Kate stood up.

"Thank you, Ben," she said. "Really. It means a lot."

"Hopefully it will mean more as we progress. But if anything, I hope that both you and Abby can rest a little easier," he said.

"I've got to get to work," he said, collecting his things.

We said goodbye.

Dr. Mortimer had done well.

Chapter 37

After Dr. Mortimer left, it took a while for us to stop talking about Nathaniel. Kate was happy that he had been found. But I wondered if that would be enough for her, if she would be able to forgive Dr. Mortimer so they could get back together.

I told her what the rafting company had told us, that the river would be closed in the morning.

"I doubt it will be for just for the morning," she said. "That entire area will be a crime scene."

She got up and put on your shoes.

"I've got to go back in for a little while," she said. "I spent most of my day arguing with Colin and didn't get much else done. But I won't be late."

"Okay. Have a good night," I said.

I checked my email. There was only one message in the inbox, from Jack reminding the team that tomorrow night's game was going to be tough and that we should meet half an hour early for extra practice.

As I watched a taped Barcelona soccer game, my thoughts drifted to Nathaniel. It was strange how things had turned out. I was sure he must be still working on his experiments. And even though I was relieved to know where he was, I still couldn't figure out why I didn't have any more visions of him murdering people.

More things I didn't understand. It seemed lately that I had a lot of those.

It took a long time before I finally fell asleep.

And then it wasn't for long.

Chapter 38

It was the noise that woke me first.

I thought it was coming from outside and jumped up, stumbling out of bed over to the window. I looked out but saw nothing. Just trees blowing and moonbeams and dancing shadows. Maybe it had been a cat, or a car passing by. I looked over at the clock. It was almost two in the morning.

And then I saw her, rising up out of the floor.

My heart pounded in terror as she stood in the corner of my bedroom. She still had that deathly serious expression and the pale, scarred face. And those intense eyes.

She stood there, somber. I started shaking uncontrollably, backing up against the far wall. What did she want from me? I was doing everything I could. The divers were going out in the morning and her body would be found. There was nothing else for me to do.

I wanted to say those things to her, but the words wouldn't come out. I could feel my eyes watering up, my breath growing shallow. I just wanted her to leave me alone.

And then she suddenly disappeared. I fell backwards into wall and slid down on the floor, trying to breathe.

Chapter 39

I drove out to the river early the next morning. The road to the take-out was closed and full of all sorts of official cars, so I went up to the next parking area. There was a trail along the river and I only had to walk about a mile or so before I saw a small crowd at the take-out down below.

I climbed up the hillside a little so I was off the path, just in case anybody was patrolling. Then I called Kate.

"So you have a good view up there?" she asked.

She had gotten access to the dive and was down there right next to the river.

"Yeah, I can see everything."

"The divers are suiting up. They'll be going in soon."

"Good," I said.

"I'll call back in a bit," she said.

About half an hour later, I watched as two divers in wet suits headed out into the water. They climbed into a small raft with one other person, and rowed to the middle of the river. Then they went in.

I sat down in a pile of dead pine needles and thought about Annabelle. I knew they would find her. I hoped it would bring her some peace. I hoped that she could move on.

In about 10 minutes, the divers came back up. Kate called a short time later.

"They found it," she said. "But like Daniel said, it's hard to get to. It'll probably take a while. You might as well go home. I'll call you with updates."

"I think I'll stick around," I said.

I wanted to stay. And be here for *her*. Kate was quiet for a moment.

"Sometimes it's just hard to believe all of this is real," she said.

"I know what you mean."

The divers swam on the surface, circling for a while, and then dove under the water with ropes. The raft hovered on the water above them. About half an hour later, the guy in the boat turned on a kind of winch.

And then she came up.

Kate called and told me they had her, in case I couldn't see. And that she was still wrapped up, just like the pictures had shown.

I watched as they brought her over to the shore and laid her up on the bank.

After eight years, Annabelle Harrison was finally out of the water.

Chapter 40

Kate was right. They ended up closing the river for the entire day and we were told not to come in to work. Ty called me right after I found out and asked if I wanted to go on the hike up to Green Lakes.

"Come on, it's a totally unexpected day off. Look, I'll invite Amber and Jake along if that would make you feel better."

But I still said no. I told him I wasn't feeling well, which was kind of true. I had barely slept the last few nights and felt exhausted. I was looking forward to a long nap.

Ty seemed okay about it, but I could tell he was a little disappointed.

"All right, call me if you change your mind."

I slept for most of the afternoon. When I got up, I saw that Kate had called. She left a message saying that they brought the body to the medical examiner's office and that she was working late, writing up the story. I called her back to check in.

"Nope, nothing else," she said. "But it's buzzing around here. It's going to be a big story. I won't be home until late."

We said goodbye and I went and checked my email. There were no messages from Claire.

I decided to go to the park to clear my head. I was still confused. As much as I liked Claire, I wasn't any closer to finding Jesse. It was getting harder and harder to quiet the doubts that were running frantic in my head, doubts that were haunting me more than Annabelle had. That voice that whispered that Jesse was gone forever.

I walked along the path in the woods searching again for him.

"I miss you so much," I said to the trees. "Where are you? Please, Jesse. Come back. Come back to me."

He wasn't on the swings where we used to have contests when we were little about who could go up the highest. He wasn't on the grass or the basketball courts. He didn't answer me.

My heart was heavy as I walked. I knew it wasn't his fault. He would be with me if he could. Nobody would choose this kind of pain.

I headed back home, feeling foolish.

I couldn't keep doing this. I couldn't spend my life searching for something that wasn't there.

***

It was a tough game. We tied it, but couldn't score again for the win. As we came off the field, Jack was doing math.

"If the Lost Boys lose tonight and the Ravens win tomorrow, we might still have a chance to make the finals."

He mumbled some more as he walked away.

When I got home, Kate was on the sofa still in her work clothes. She looked tired. Her hair was up but in a mess and her eyes had dark circles under them.

"Abby, there you are," she said. "I totally forgot you had soccer tonight. How'd it go?"

"We tied," I said, pulling off my cleats.

I sat down next to her.

"How'd it go today?" I asked.

"Good. Just a hell of a long day," she said, rubbing her face. "But you did it. They found the body and should have a positive ID in the next few weeks. It's gotta be Annabelle."

"Good," I said. "Now she can move on. We can all move on."

"I still can't believe all this, that you see spirits and ghosts," Kate said. "Doesn't it scare you? I wouldn't want to see dead people. It's hard enough dealing with the living."

I shrugged.

"Yeah," I said. "But I don't have a choice whether to see them or not. At least, I didn't with her. But I wish she could have given us some sort of clue about the killer. It's kind of frustrating that we don't know."

"I guess real life has to step in somewhere along the line. It would be too much to expect her to have some incriminating evidence on her that would lead directly to the murderer. Or for her to walk up to the killer and point a ghostly finger. But the cops might get lucky," Kate said. "Look at all those Cold Case Files they solve on TV. There must be evidence they can check through again."

"I hope so," I said.

Kate nodded and yawned.

"I'm turning in early tonight," she said. "I've gotta get some sleep."

Chapter 41

The river was open the next day and I was happy to get back to work. On the way up to the launch, everyone was talking about the body and who it could be. Amber thought it was a woman who disappeared last year. Jake guessed it was the fisherman who fell out of his boat and disappeared up at the dam at the beginning of the summer.

"I wonder when they'll release the name," Jake asked.

"Depends," Ty said. "If there's no ID on the body, then they'll have to do DNA tests and dental records and all that."

I was quiet. I was tired of thinking about bodies and death and ghosts. I looked out at the trees as we drove along the highway.

Ty hadn't said much to me and I hoped he wasn't angry about the hike.

"So what did you end up doing yesterday?" I asked while we unloaded gear and waited for the bus of customers.

Ty looked up at me, but seemed kind of sad.

"Laundry. A bike ride. Took my dog to the park. Not much."

I smiled, but he turned and walked away.

I wanted to talk to him, but I couldn't do it quite yet. I needed the right words and I was still figuring it all out.

As I paddled and steered through the rapids on the last run, I looked around at the tall trees and black lava rocks and the rushing water. A strong whiff of pine was blowing around. The sun was warm.

Such a beautiful place for such terrible sadness.

Chapter 42

It had been two weeks since they had pulled up Annabelle, and she still hadn't been identified. It was a big story though, and Kate was on the front page a lot. On Saturday afternoon, she sent me a text asking if I could meet her at Mondo for dinner. She had been working nonstop at the paper lately and I had barely seen her. Pizza sounded good. I drove over about six, got us a table, and waited.

I hadn't seen the ghost of Annabelle since that night she came to my room. Not on the cliffs, not by the river, not at the park. I was hoping she was appeased, if not at peace, and that she had watched as they pulled her body out of her watery grave. I was hoping it was enough for her.

Kate walked in, the screen door slamming behind her. She sat down in the rickety chair across from me.

"Hey, Abby. What do you want? It's on me."

"Cheese, please," I said.

She went up to the counter, ordered, and came back with two slices on paper plates while I got the water. I grabbed my pizza and started stuffing it in my face. I hadn't eaten all day and was ravenous.

"Thanks," I said when I was nearly finished.

"Sure."

I wiped my face with a napkin and leaned back, suddenly full.

"So, is it strange to be working with Colin now?" I asked.

Kate had broken up with him the week before.

"Yeah, a little," she said. "He's been giving me weird looks, but I'm getting used to it. No, I can't say I'm comfortable working with him, but whatever. In the future I'll pay more attention to that advice about office romances. About not fishing off the company pier and stuff."

She had told me that the breakup had nothing to do with Dr. Mortimer. But I wasn't sure about that. At the very least, after hanging out with him, Kate would have been reminded how she really should be feeling about her boyfriend.

I watched as more people jammed into the small pizza place. A huge line was forming up at the counter.

I finished my water.

"I'm getting another slice," Kate said. "Want one?"

I shook my head.

She was in line for a while, but finally showed up with a large slice with the works. The pungent smell of onions and garlic closed in around us.

"So you think that you and Claire are done with Annabelle Harrison?" Kate asked.

I had told her about Claire a few nights earlier when she came home late and found me on the computer reading her website. I figured I might as well come clean and just tell her, even if she would make fun of me. But I was surprised by her reaction. She looked through the site with a serious expression, and even spent some time reading Claire's biography.

"I'm hoping it's the last of Annabelle," I said. "My part is done. She's been found."

"I still have trouble believing in all that stuff."

169

She finished and got up, throwing away the trash. I saw that there was a sea of gray mist surrounding her. She was nervous about something.

She grabbed her plastic glass and sucked on the straw.

"I got a job interview back East," she said. "New York."

My stomach tightened.

"Wow," I said finally. "That's great."

"The telephone interview is on Thursday. If that goes well then they'll invite me to go out there for a real interview with the higher ups in a couple of weeks."

"Of course it'll go well," I said.

"I've been at *The Bugler* a while now and if I'm going to move up in this business, I need to break through now. I haven't decided anything yet, even if they offer me something. But I wanted you to know."

The Cure's *Fascination Street* vibrated through Mondo as I sat thinking about Kate moving away. We had never been apart before and although I should have been happy for her, I was mostly feeling freaked out. I didn't want her to go.

"You could come with me," she said. "Or you can stay here in Bend, keep living in our house. It's almost paid for, so you don't have to worry about that. And I'll come back to visit often."

I tried to smile, but couldn't. I tried to keep my eyes from filling up, but I couldn't do that either.

"You deserve it. Really. I'm glad you're focusing on your career."

But as I said those words, I was breaking apart inside.

Kate looked at me.

"We'll find a way to make it work. I promise."

"Have you told Dr. Mortimer?"

I already knew the answer. I think I would have felt his sadness radiating all the way from the hospital if he knew.

"No," Kate said. "Not yet. But he must remember that I had applications out. When we were dating I always talked about leaving Bend and going to a city to write important stories."

"Annabelle's story was important," I said.

"Yeah, I know. But that was a fluke. That's not your usual Bend story about the city council voting to kill all the geese because there's too much poop in the park. That's much more the norm."

It was true. It was a hot debate at City Hall last year and Kate wrote a lot about it.

"I'll miss you," I said. "But I want you to be happy. It's like Erin says. If staying here isn't what you want, then you need to leave. You belong at *The New York Times*."

"Thanks, Abby," she said.

I thought I saw tears in her eyes too, but she looked away quickly. She got up and I followed her outside as we headed over to her car.

"See you later tonight," she said.

I waved goodbye.

I walked down Franklin and crossed over to the park. I looked anyway even though I knew that I wouldn't find him. I checked in the trees across the water and in the shadows along the banks.

I was always losing the people I loved, one way or another.

I cried all the way home.

Chapter 43

A little more than a week later the authorities officially identified the body they had pulled out of the bottom of the Deschutes River as Annabelle Harrison. They also announced that the cause of death was a blunt force to the back of the head.

"You were right again. It was murder," Kate said, as we watched the news coverage on television one night. She had been writing up all the stories related to Annabelle and continued to dominate the front page of *The Bugler*. A few of her stories had been picked up by some of the newspapers around the state as well as the Associated Press.

We had seen several clips already of Derek and Jacob Harrison talking to the media, microphones pushed up in their faces. Derek Harrison called the discovery "heartbreaking" and told reporters that they were planning a memorial service so that "Annabelle could be properly laid to rest." Her son mostly stayed in the background, but one time he stepped up and said that it was good to finally know what really happened to his mom.

It was heartwarming seeing her son. And as I watched him I realized that I had helped him a little. That was at least one small consolation that had come out of this horrible tragedy: whether or not they found the murderer, he would now always know that his mother had not abandoned him. Maybe that wasn't such a small thing.

The summer had flown and somehow I had only one more week left on the river. Ty and Amber would still be working through the end of September, but soon after Labor Day the company cut back on the daily runs and I would be out of a job.

I was going to miss the river and being outside on it every day. I had no idea what I would do, but I was sure it would be hard to find anything that would give me that sense of peace.

The party I was planning never happened. Dr. Mortimer canceled a few days before, Kate was only thinking about New York, and Jack and Tim from the soccer team always seemed to be busy. And with no job on the horizon, I didn't exactly have much money to spend on a party anyway.

I was putting in applications in stores and coffee shops all over town, but so far had no luck finding anything. But I wasn't too worried. I figured something would open up for me soon.

Dr. Mortimer called Thursday, asking if I could stop by and talk on his dinner break. I was supposed to meet Ty at eight over at McMenamins, so I told him I could swing over by the hospital beforehand.

I found him in the ER waiting room, sitting off in a corner. He was in his scrubs, slouching in a plastic chair when I walked up. He looked serious and sad. I knew Kate must have told him the news.

"Hi, Abby," he said.

We walked over to the elevators and went upstairs to the orthopedic section of the hospital. It was closed, so no one was on the floor. The chairs were big and cushioned and comfortable.

"So she told you, huh?" I said.

"Yeah."

He brushed his hand though his thick hair and through the turbulent darkness moving above him.

"It's just a surprise, is all. I don't know why. I just wasn't thinking. She's wanted this for a long time."

"I was surprised too," I said.

He looked different, much different than I'd ever seen before. Kate's news had rocked him hard. He was intense and sad and something else I couldn't put my finger on. He leaned back, crossing his feet out in front of him.

"She's not leaving for the interview until Tuesday," I said. "Do you have plans to see her before she goes?"

"No," he said, his eyes darting around the waiting room. "Can't."

I smiled nervously.

"No soccer tonight?"

"No, we finished up the outdoor league. But indoor starts on Monday. New team with a lot of the same players. It'll be fun."

"I'll come watch one of those games too."

"Sounds good," I said, trying to fill up the strange silence.

"I want to tell you something but you have to promise not to tell Kate. Can you do that?"

"Sure."

He sighed nervously.

"I'm leaving for Kenya tomorrow. I'm going to confront Nathaniel."

My heart raced. No wonder his energy was wild and dark. I didn't know how to respond.

"But Dr. Mortimer, you shouldn't...." I started to say, but he must have seen the terror in my eyes and cut me off.

"No, Abby. Don't say it. I'm going. It's all set. I've taken time off here at the hospital and have my ticket already."

"Okay," I said.

"Look, I just needed you to know, that's all. I have to find him and take care of this situation."

I understood, but I still didn't want him to go.

"He's a dangerous man, Dr. Mortimer. You have to be careful."

He rubbed his face. It looked like he hadn't slept in a week.

"I know. Don't worry about me. He's my brother. Besides, I understand now who he is and what he's capable of doing. I didn't get that before, but now I do. I'm ready. Now I have the upper hand."

I couldn't imagine anyone ever having the upper hand when confronting Nathaniel Mortimer. It would be like playing a chess game against Bobby Fischer—a crazy, murderous Bobby Fischer. He was always a few moves ahead, waiting patiently on the other side of sanity.

"Just be careful," I said again.

He suddenly stood up.

"Sorry, I have to get back. Don't tell her, Abby. I'll be in contact with you through email and I promise to keep you updated."

We hugged.

"Bye," I said. "Please be careful."

We pulled away and he ran down the stairs.

I left the hospital wondering if I would ever see him again.

Chapter 44

I drove over to meet Ty and tried to figure out what to do. It was an impossible situation. If I told Kate that Dr. Mortimer was leaving for Africa, he would be mad. And if I didn't tell her, she would be mad.

I pulled up and found Ty waiting in the parking lot. We said hello and then went inside and grabbed a table.

It was good to see him. As always, he looked great.

We talked about the weather and about and the end of the year party that the rafting company was planning when the season officially closed in a few weeks.

"So you miss being out on the river all day?" he asked.

"Yeah," I said. "More than I even thought I would."

I told him about my unsuccessful job hunt and how I had been looking everywhere, including Starbucks, Macy's, and all the outlet stores.

"You gotta think of something else. You won't be happy in any of those places. What about working up at the mountain? I know you said you weren't ready to be an instructor, but what about a manager or something? They're hiring and I could put in a word for you."

I smiled. I couldn't imagine telling Kate that I'd be driving up to Mt. Bachelor all winter, on the same road where I had the accident.

"I better pass this season," I said. "But thanks anyway."

"Are you coming back as a guide next summer?" he asked.

"I'd like to. They told me they wanted me back."

I hoped that whatever I ended up doing, I could always go back and be a guide in the summers.

"It was a great season," Ty said.

"To our summer on the river," I said, picking up my glass.

We toasted.

As the night went on, we talked about more and more things. Ty switched to beers and loosened up a bit.

"So, Abby, how come we never went on that hike? I just want to know. Obviously, I'm interested in you. Just tell me if you don't feel the same way. It won't be a big deal. Promise."

I had been thinking about what to say to him for weeks.

"Well, it just scares me. I really like you, Ty, but don't know if I'm ready. I love having you as a friend. I know that's not fair to you if that's all there ever will be. And I'm not sure if it can be anything more."

"Let me decide what's fair," he said. "I can handle it. That works for me now."

He looked at me for a minute.

"Let's just hang out together and see what happens," he finally said.

We sat in silence and finished our drinks.

"Okay, Abby Craig," Ty said as we walked back to the cars. The night air was cold on my face. "I'll be around. How about you call me if you feel like it? We can go see a movie or take a walk. I'm a pretty good goalie too, if you want to get in some practice. You just let me know."

He leaned over and kissed me on the cheek. He still smelled of that tropical lotion that he rubbed on his skin all summer.

"Okay," I said, smiling. "Deal."

I watched as he walked away.

Chapter 45

Kate pulled out her suitcase and threw it on the bed.

"You know, normally I wouldn't mind, but he's been such a jerk lately," she said.

She was leaving for New York in the morning and the editors had decided that Colin would be taking over her beat while she was gone, which meant he was going to be writing up a lot of the top stories.

We were in her room and I was lying on the floor with her fluffy down comforter over me.

"Let it go, Kate. Who cares? Look where you're going and what you're doing. You're leaving for an interview in New York City."

She put the three piles of clothes on her desk inside the carry-on. Then she grabbed a few more sweaters and stuffed them in. She was only going for a few days, but seemed to be packing for a month.

"I still have to get the job remember. I'm still up against a lot of people. A lot of topnotch people."

"I think Annabelle's story is going to push you right past all the competition."

"Thanks. Hey, speaking of Annabelle, I called the Portland detectives today. They opened up her case again and now it's a homicide. I'm really hoping they take a good look at her husband again."

I had watched Harrison on television. I knew it wasn't him.

"I don't think he did it," I said.

"Really?"

"Just a feeling."

I sighed and was quiet.

"Abby, finding Annabelle should make you feel really good. You helped them. Both of them."

"*We* helped them," I said. "It does feel good, but I want more. I want them to find out who killed her. I just wish she could have told me who did it. I hate that there's still a killer out there."

Kate took another jacket out of her closet and put it on the bed.

"You're starting to remind me of some of those cops I deal with," she said. "The ones who have been at it a while, have a heaviness inside that only seems to get worse with the weight of every unsolved case."

"Hmmm," I said.

"But these things take time. It's just the beginning of the investigation," she said. "I'm hoping they'll leave me out of it though."

"What do you mean?"

"I got a call from Bend PD. They heard that I was in Portland, snooping around about Annabelle a week before Daniel took his pictures of the body. They're a little suspicious and want me to come in and talk to them."

"Damn," I said. "You should have told me sooner."

"This kind of stuff comes with the job. Don't worry. I'm not worried. If I have to, I'll tell them I have an anonymous source who tipped me off. But I'm hoping they'll leave it alone."

I told Kate I didn't care if she had to tell them about me, about how I saw Annabelle's ghost. I was tired of hiding.

Maybe it was time to just be who I was and not care what other people thought.

"Just tell them. I don't care."

"Thanks, but nobody's going to believe your ghost story anyway. I'm glad you're thinking along those lines though. It's time for you to be comfortable in your skin."

We were quiet for a while. Kate sat on the suitcase and I helped her zip it up.

"I just wish Ben was in town," she said.

Dr. Mortimer told her that he was in California at a medical convention for the week and that he might stay on a little longer to visit family.

"Even though we know that someone is watching Nathaniel, I still hate to leave you alone."

"I'm fine. Really. Don't worry about that. I have some friends around if I need anything. So if they offer you the job when would you start?"

"Within the month. But let's not get ahead of ourselves."

I smiled.

"Kate. If it's good, I want you to take it. Really. I'll be disappointed if you don't." I looked at her for a minute. "I'm serious. And like you said, you'll come back to visit. And I'll come visit too. It's important to do what we're supposed to do. You've outgrown The Bugler. You need to move on."

Kate reached over and gave me a long hug.

"And I'll even keep watering your flowers."

It was a pretty good joke and I was glad to see her laugh. Almost all her flowers had died in a freak early frost the week before.

"Thanks, Abby. It means a lot that you're supporting me."

We said goodnight. Her flight was early and I was dropping her off at the Redmond airport in just a few hours.

Chapter 46

Shortly after Kate left, I started a new job at Back Street Coffee. I was just working at the counter, but so far it was okay. I liked the people. They were friendly.

Ty had already stopped by a few times. He sat up at the bar and always ordered a black coffee.

Kate had called Wednesday in the afternoon and left a message saying that the interview had gone well. I called her on my break and she told me that they had asked her back for one last interview later in the week.

"That sounds like a good sign," I said.

I was standing in the alley, wishing I had my jacket. A breeze was blowing right into me.

"Yeah," Kate said. "It does, huh?"

I didn't tell her, but I had a strong feeling that she would be offered the job. And I was finally okay with it. I was learning to accept change.

I finished my shift and grabbed my stuff in the back. The owner, Mike, was up on a ladder, hoisting a large burlap bag off a shelf.

"Bye, Mike," I said, taking off my apron and hanging it up on the rack.

"See you tomorrow, Abby."

It wasn't that late yet, but the sun didn't seem as bright and was already falling out of the sky. It was hard to get used to it, summer slipping away and autumn coming. But some of the leaves were already changing and there was a nip in the air.

I walked down Bond Street and then over to the library to return some books for Kate.

***

It was busy downtown. People were out eating in restaurants and going to the bank and buying jewelry. They were walking their dogs and making deliveries and trying on clothes in the boutiques. They were working and eating and laughing.

And I was dropping books off at the library.

That's when I saw him.

In the trees by the parking lot, standing there, watching me.

I jumped at first, my heart thundering hard and fast in my chest. My breath disappeared. Tears welled up fast in my eyes.

It couldn't be him.

But he kept staring as he walked toward me. He was still wearing that damn baseball cap.

It was him.

"Hey, Craigers," he said, coming in close.

I looked up into his gray eyes. He didn't look away. I couldn't move.

Jesse.

Chapter 47

I couldn't stop crying.

He was in front of me.

Standing right there.

I reached out and touched his face.

Jesse.

I was frozen. Confused. Breathless. I couldn't stop staring at him.

"Craigers, you gotta say something," he said. "And you gotta breathe."

He didn't look any different. He was exactly the same as I remembered.

I was spinning.

"Jesse?" I finally whispered, forcing the words out. "Is it really you?"

"Yeah, it's me, Craigers." He gave me a long hug. "Please. I know you're in shock. But come with me. I need to talk to you and I don't have much time."

He took my hand and we walked over to the park, found a bench, and sat down.

"I can't believe this," I said.

My head was light. I couldn't think straight.

"Come on, Craigers, you've seen ghosts before. It's not so crazy."

He laughed a little, but then was serious again.

"But where have you been?" I asked.

We embraced and I was lost inside him and never wanted to let go. He smelled the same, felt the same. And I felt safe in his arms.

A harsh wind blew into us. It was true. He was real. Jesse was real.

I touched his face again, my fingers sliding down over his lips.

"I remember our kiss at the lake. I love you, Jesse. I want you to know that."

"I know that, Craigers. I love you too."

He stood up.

"But something's coming," he said. "That's why I'm here. There's a darkness gathering around you."

"What are you talking about?"

"I don't know exactly," he said, sitting back down. "You don't see it, do you?"

"No," I said. "I don't."

Two women walked by with a little dog.

"Is it Annabelle? Is she coming back?"

"Let's walk for a while," he said.

I smiled as he took my hand and pulled me up. It was the same Jesse. Never able to sit for long. I was surprised he didn't have his basketball.

We walked alongside the river. He put his arm around me and pulled me tight as we headed over to the bridge, the wind blowing dead leaves into us.

"I've missed you."

"I've missed you too, Craigers," he said. "But I had to leave."

"I know," I said. "I figured they wouldn't let you stay. It killed me, though."

Jesse was quiet. We walked up to the middle of the bridge and looked out at the river. It was windy, but we stood watching the ducks swim by, watching the trees blow.

"I'm sorry, Craigers. But it was the only way."

I inhaled, the air stinging my lungs. The sun was nearly gone now but there was still a lightness in the sky.

"Wait," I said. "What do you mean, it was the only way?"

He looked at me, his sad eyes large.

"You needed to move on. You couldn't live your life being in love with… with whatever it is I am now. I had to leave."

I pulled my hand away.

"You're saying you had a choice?"

Jesse was quiet. I started shivering. It was cold. And what he was saying made me feel even colder.

"I did it for you, Craigers. I did it because I love you."

I looked up at him. Anger, hot and quick, shot through me.

"That's not love. Leaving isn't love, Jesse."

We stood apart, quiet. I tried to calm down.

"It was for the best," he said, moving closer. "And it wasn't easy, Craigers. Do you know how hard it's been, being away from you? Do you know how much I love you still? But there wasn't a choice. Not a real one anyway. You can't give your life over to a ghost. Staying away was the right thing to do. I did it for you."

I moved a few steps away.

"It's been hell without you here. You're saying you left me on purpose, that you could have stayed?"

Jesse played with his hat, pushing it down tight on his head. I walked off the bridge and he followed.

"Craigers," he said. "It's like I told you back at the lake, you don't need me anymore."

"How could you say that? I'll always need you."

My face was hot with fury, the tears flowing from my eyes. I walked up ahead of him. He could have been with me this whole time. But he had chosen instead to break my heart.

I turned around. I wanted to hear his explanation, I wanted to hear why.

But he was gone.

Again.

I ran, ran until I couldn't think anymore. Ran up a steep hill, ran until his voice was pounded out of my mind and I only heard my hard breathing in the night air.

I didn't know where I was going and I didn't care. When I stopped, I stared out at the lights twinkling in the city below me and screamed.

I tried to push him out of my mind. He left me when he didn't have to. He had decided our future and had taken that choice away from me.

I would have loved a ghost. And I would have loved him forever. I *would* love him forever.

"Damn it, Jesse," I whispered into the darkness.

When there were no more tears left, I started back. I walked in a daze down the hill, past the bridge, and then to the Jeep.

I didn't see Jesse in the parking lot.

And I didn't want to.

Chapter 48

It took me a few days to realize that Jesse was right. My anger was gone and replaced by a searing guilt that kept me up at night. I was wrong for getting so angry at him for doing what was best for us. Maybe one day we could be together, but not now. I couldn't be in his world and he knew it was wrong to stay in mine.

I had acted like a child.

I was glad that I had the job and was working a lot of hours. It helped me get my mind off everything.

I wanted to see him, even if it was just once more.

Only to say that I was sorry.

***

I looked for him over at our park in the morning and then at the library on the way to work. On my break, I walked around downtown hoping to bump into him. I whispered my apologies in the wind, hoping they would reach his ears even if he didn't come back.

I knew now that he still loved me and that it must have been hard to stay away.

I also realized too that I hadn't completely healed from the accident. I still had to let go of Jesse's ghost. That would be the last and hardest part.

I wandered back over to Back Street. I still had 10 minutes left on my break and sat outside at one of the tables and checked my phone. Kate had called and left a long message saying they had taken her out sightseeing and she had seen the Statue of Liberty and the World Trade Center Memorial.

Jack Martin had called too, reminding me about our indoor game that night.

I inhaled and ignored my jittery stomach. I stared at the numbers on my phone. And then I called Ty.

He didn't pick up, but I left a message inviting him out to dinner on Friday night. My treat.

I walked back in and finished my shift, feeling a little better.

Chapter 49

I drove over to the indoor soccer arena thinking about the plastic turf. In our last game, I had gotten a nasty burn when I was pushed down by a crazy girl with long hair. This was the first season I had ever played indoors. It was fun and all, but nothing like real soccer.

I turned on Empire and pulled up to the large warehouse. It was nice seeing the familiar cars in the parking lot. I zipped up my jacket as I walked toward the doors. The stars were out, bright in the cool black sky above.

It was an easy win, 3-1. I scored one of the goals with Tim's help.

Jack handed out Gatorades to celebrate the win. I finished most of it, grabbed my stuff, and then headed out.

My heart raced as I looked out in the parking lot. Jesse was by the lights. He had come back and I had another chance.

"Jesse," I said, running up to him.

He smiled when I looked back up at him. He still didn't look like a ghost.

"I'm so sorry," I said. "I totally overreacted. It's just that I've missed you so much."

"I know, Craigers," he said, looking at me. "I understand. You have to know that I did it because I love you. More than ever."

"I know that now," I said.

"But I've come back for another reason."

"What?"

"The black energy—"

Cars drove by, their headlights like spotlights.

Jack suddenly walked up.

"Good game," he said. "Good night."

He didn't see Jesse. I could tell. I smiled. But when I turned back, Jesse was gone.

I knew he would come back. And when he did, we would figure it out. We would find a way to make it work.

***

The Jeep wouldn't start.

I tried it again as Jack walked back over.

"That doesn't sound good. What's up?"

"I don't know," I said. "It's not starting."

"Probably just the battery. Let me grab my cables."

The parking lot was nearly empty now and Jack moved his truck over to the Jeep. He hooked up the two cars and we tried to get it going. But it still wouldn't turn over.

"Let me try one last thing," he said.

He fiddled with something else as the last car left. But it was no use.

"I'll run you home, Abby," he said, smiling. "No big deal. We can come back with a new battery in the morning."

"Okay," I said. "That would be great."

Chapter 50

It must have been in the Gatorade bottle that Jack handed to me after the game.

I had been in and out of consciousness for hours.

"I feel sick," I mumbled.

"You'll be okay, Abby. Just relax. That's the best thing you can do for yourself right now."

I was in the backseat, tied down. Jack was driving. It was dark. Dark and empty.

The lights of the highway fluttered by like in a dream. My mind was heavy. Fuzzy. But I knew that if I had any chance to save myself, I had to remember the landmarks. I had to stay awake and pay attention to where he was taking me.

We drove for hours. I tried to hang on to the things we passed. The neon reindeer sign in Portland. The Columbia River crossing into Washington. The Space Needle.

Heavy metal drilled through the car and into my throbbing head. My wrists ached.

"Jack, what are you doing?" I asked, still groggy and nauseous. "Where are you taking me?"

"I'm just the courier," he said. "Bringing you from Point A to Point B. Everything will be fine. Like I said, you just need to relax."

We drove on in the dark. I was tired and then I let go, falling away with the distant lonely sound of foghorns lulling me into a deep sleep.

When I woke again, we were moving, but not moving. It was lighter out, but dull. I looked out the window. Rain poured down from the sky onto the water.

Another foghorn.

We were on a ferry.

I caught his eyes in the rearview mirror, watching me.

"Who the hell are you?" I said.

"I'm a doctor, Abby. I specialize in research."

He leaned over the seat and put duct tape over my mouth and pushed me down on the floor.

"Even this early there are a lot of people on this ferry. Wouldn't want you to call out and spoil things."

My heart raced.

"He's excited to see you," he said. "He can't wait. He's flying in tomorrow."

Nathaniel.

He was delivering me to Nathaniel.

44 Book Three

coming Valentine's Day 2012

ABOUT THE AUTHOR

Like her main character, Jools Sinclair lives in Bend, Oregon. She is currently working on *44 Book Three*.

Learn more about Jools Sinclair
and the *44* series at
JoolsSinclair44.blogspot.com